MW01133337

PENTIMENTO

by
Cameron Jace

www.CameronJace.com

Edited by Jami Hampson

Merriam-webster's definition of **pen-ti-men-to**:
An underlying image in a painting, as an earlier painting, part of a painting, or original draft, that shows through, usually when the top layer of paint has become transparent with age. From pentire, which means to repent in Italian.

1

Iris Beaumont wondered if the boy she had a crush on was one of the Beasts. Although he was seventeen, he didn't look his age. He was a hunk, more tall and slender than most boys, with a body of a twenty-four-year-old athlete. His eyes were a sparkling blue, like late night ocean waves under a full moon. Naturally, he owned a demanding voice, and he was the school's best steelball player. All nine yards of clichés in one boy. Colton Ray was just too good to be true. He had to be one of the Beasts.

Iris, his total opposite, was dangling her bare feet from the edge of the principal's rooftop. Munching on a chocolate bar, she watched him walking gracefully in the schoolyard, as if he were king of the world. It was a fabulous scene. Real, yet dreamy. She let a sigh escape her lips and took another bite. The worst thing about this was watching the queen bee, Eva Washington, holding her king's hand then kiss him briefly as they strolled on.

"We really shouldn't be up here," puffed Zoe, sitting next to her best friend. She was trying not to look down or she'd get dizzy.

Iris didn't reply, chewing slower on the chocolate, imagining it was Eva screaming between her teeth.

"Do you have any idea how much trouble you're into already?" Zoe began her parental speech. "You always skip class and risk being expelled while you know it's our last year before college," she counted on her fingers. "Last week you left school, manipulating the security robots somehow. And now you drag me up here, right above the principal's office, to watch Colton. He doesn't even know you exist, by the way."

"Don't you think he deserves better?" Iris discarded Zoe's advice. The best way to make their friendship work was not taking Zoe seriously.

"Better? Are you kidding me?" Zoe said. Iris saw her fight the temptation to look down and double check on the most beautiful couple in school. "She is one of the most gorgeous girls in the school."

"Is that all boys look for in a girl, beauty?" Iris let the chocolate melt on her tongue. She suddenly wished she was a fire-breathing dragon that could devour Eva in one jealously-filled bite. It wasn't a wicked thought. Iris would never hurt anyone. She just liked Colton immensely--even when she suspected he was one of the Beasts. If he'd only notice her, she'd show him she was a special girl.

"Not all boys," Zoe said. "But most of them."

"I don't think boys are shallow or narrow-minded," Iris said. "It's just that they're made to think a beautiful girl is what they need. Look at Colton down there. Is it only me who thinks he is pretending he likes Eva? I mean, she does all the talk and he is smiling like a statue. It's as if he is some kind of politician. He isn't really happy with her. He is just pretending to be."

"I hate to burst your bubble, Iris," Zoe said. "But you're saying this because you're jealous of Eva. You secretly wish she'd disappear. Poof in the wind."

"Or she'd be taken by the Beasts," Iris said spontaneously.

Zoe shrieked immediately. "How could you say that?" her eyes darted sideways, making sure no one heard her friend.

Iris turned to face Zoe with the bar of chocolate between her teeth. Her eyes were a little moistened. She'd suddenly realized the predicament of her words. "I'm sorry. I didn't mean it like that. I didn't really mean that I hoped Eva would be taken as a Bride for the Beasts." The chocolate bar fell in her lap. "You know I don't like to keep my thoughts trapped inside my head. I just say what I feel."

"But that was mean," Zoe, always playing Iris's seventeen-year-old mother, folded her arms, even though she didn't even like Eva. But such a wish was beyond ethics. "The last thing any of us wants is to be taken by the Beasts. Isn't it enough that one of us *has* to be taken every once in a while, and we can't do anything about it?"

"I'm sorry, mommy," Iris rolled her eyes. Apologizing once was politeness. Expected to keep apologizing was stupidity. "It was just a slip of the tongue." She gazed up at the metallic skyscrapers in the distance, watching them thrusting through the sky like daggers. The sun was unusually high, splaying its rays upon the silvery city. Iris didn't know why she didn't like her city. Still, whenever her eyes darted upwards, she couldn't stop looking. She suspected the Beasts lived somewhere up there in the clouds.

"Don't you dare distract me by looking so dazed and confused at the city like you always do," Zoe pulled her head gently down.

"I didn't mean that either, Zoe." Iris said. "You know I just get distracted when I look up there." Although Iris was a citizen of The Second United States of America, she couldn't help but feel like a stranger in a strange land.

"Then don't look up when I am talking to you." Zoe commented. "You know that..." she stopped suddenly to Eva's pitched laugh from far below. Eva had a lingering voice that boys, and some girls, liked a lot. Zoe pretended not to be a fan, but she was. Most girls wished they could act as elegantly as she did.

Iris gazed back down at Colton and Eva, the happiest faces in school. They were like movie stars, always surrounded by their fans. This time, Iris tried to be honest with herself. Eva was beautiful. The kind of beauty that Iris never wished to possess, because if she did, she'd be self-conscious and scared to look in a mirror in case one simple feature changed a tiny bit. Iris had noticed that about most beautiful girls when she met them in the bathroom. Although they usually ignored her, she noticed how the slightest misshape in their faces was like the end of the world, leading her to wonder if beauty was some kind of a curse.

"So do you think Colton is one of the Beasts?" Iris snickered.

"He is definitely a sexy beast," Zoe giggled, adjusting her glasses.

"And you think I'm horrible," Iris giggled back. "But I don't mean it like that. You know what I mean."

Zoe shrugged and leaned away from Iris. Although best friends, it was ironic that Zoe preferred to stay out of trouble. "He can't be a Beast," she whispered, her eyes darting around again. "No one has ever seen the Beasts. No one, but the Council."

"Do you really believe that?" Iris wondered why they were whispering. Did the Beasts have eyes and ears in the sky? "I mean, maybe the Beasts want us to think they're invisible. Maybe they live among us, disguised in beautiful boys, like Colton."

"Can't be," Zoe shook her head. Although she liked to follow the rules, she couldn't resist talking about the mysterious Beasts who ruled The Second United States. Actually, most teenagers were curious. But only a few like Iris brought up the subject without fear. "If the Beasts could manipulate their image in any way, they wouldn't need to take a girl from us every now and then. It's very obvious they are hideous looking. They might have the technology that saved the planet and provides us with all our needs, but we don't call them Beasts for nothing." replied Zoe.

"That's my girl," Iris smiled. "Although I'm not sure I agree with you, once you let go and say what you want, I like you more. You have to practice being pissed off and expressive like that often."

Zoe adjusted her glasses. "Do you think so?" she said.

Iris nodded.

"I'm afraid boys like Colton won't like me if I express myself," Zoe said. "My mom told me so."

"Boys like Colton," Iris sighed. "Won't like us either way."

Iris and Zoe stared down at Colton and Eva kissing in the middle of the schoolyard. Watching them, the two best friends began sighing in unison. Iris envied Eva for tasting Colton lips, and imagined hers on his instead. Her only distraction was watching Zoe on the verge of clapping and applauding Colton's performance. It was a long kiss, and almost everyone around was witnessing it. Such an entrancing scene.

Suddenly, in the middle of this, something terrifying happened.

A horn blared in the distance.

2

The horn was extremely loud. It was heard all over the city, as if a giant burped in the sky. But its loudness wasn't the only scary thing about it. What the blasting of the horn meant raised goosebumps on every seventeen-year-old girl's skin in The Second.

Iris watched Eva and Colton's lips part, as a dreadful look dimmed Eva's face. Iris's too. She stared back at Zoe with wide eyes. Zoe looked like she was going to faint, and Iris's heartbeat sprang to the roof. It was the horn they all feared. They called it the Call of the Beast. One miserable and unlucky girl was going to be *Called* right now, and never seen again.

The horn was always followed by the beeping of everyone's phones. Iris watched Zoe's hand shake while holding her vibrating phone. The beep was a message with one of the girls' IDs. The one girl the Beasts were going to take tonight. It was said that the Beasts liked to call her the Bride.

Zoe shivered, pulling the phone up to eye level. Iris heard the other girls' phones beep down in the schoolyard. The beeps never came at once. There was always this slight delay between beeps, as if to make sure the tension never died. Finally, Iris's phone beeped.

Iris wasn't going to push the button. She'd always let Zoe push hers and then tell her. Iris couldn't bring herself to do it. What if the girl's ID turned out to be hers?

Down on school grounds, a number of girls were congratulating each other. Although it was one girl's ill-fated day, all uncalled girls couldn't help but celebrate--at least until the next Call.

Looking at the girls, Iris caught Colton look up in her direction. She thought it must have been her beeping phone that made him notice her. From this far, she could see his blue eyes still sparkling. He seemed amused by the girl dangling her bare feet from the principal's rooftop. For a brief and awkward moment, their eyes locked.

Everything was happening fast, Iris thought this was too much for her. Both the terrifying horn and Colton's lovely blue eyes catching hers, as if she were a fallen star. Gosh, she'd been waiting for him to notice her since forever. Why did he have to choose such an awkward moment?

Iris broke Colton's gaze to Zoe's shriek. Something she only did when she was happy or sad.

"It's not me!" Zoe yelled. "It's not me!"

Iris was happy for her, but she was about to kill her nonetheless. Shouldn't Zoe tell her if it wasn't her ID too? "But..." Zoe slowly lifted her head to meet her best friend's eyes. A sympathizing look filled Zoe's eyes, as if she'd just lost her speech.

"What is it?" Iris shook Zoe by the shoulder. Zoe was tongue-tied, staring at Iris as if she were a ghost.

This wasn't happening, Iris thought. It couldn't be me. I'm not ready for this. I am not ready to be taken by the Beasts.

Iris pulled her hands off of Zoe and pushed the button on her phone to check the message for herself, but the phone fell in her lap. Her hands were shivering. It couldn't be her. She stretched her hand to pick up the phone again. It didn't make sense. She didn't deserve this. She had plans in her life. Big plans, with Colton hopefully part of them. Iris was planning to be become a painter, a special kind of painter, and a great one. She hadn't been given the name Iris for nothing. Her dad claimed he knew she was going to have a peculiar eye that could see through things, eyes that would capture the moment and the feeling, then paint them on canvas. And even if she failed at this, she'd always known she was special, only she didn't know how. If the Beasts took her today, how was she going to know what she could have accomplished? And why was this happening right after Colton noticed her for the first time? This was so unfair.

The thoughts were heavy on her, like a big weight on her shoulders. As she tried to pick up the phone again, it slipped from her hand. Again. This time it spiraled downward, way below, to the school grounds. Her heart almost fell to her toes with it. Her back arched, and she was about to jump after her phone. If Zoe was afraid to tell her, how would she know now?

Her eyes met Colton's again, staring upward at the falling phone. He raised his eyes again at the barefoot girl dangling her feet from the principal's rooftop. Colton's eyes were locked with hers in that brief and awkward moment again. Suddenly, everything stopped in the world around Iris. She couldn't hear the celebrating girls anymore. And if Zoe had gained her speech, she couldn't hear her either. She could only see one face. The face of the boy who never knew she existed before. Now he knew about her, and she thought he looked interested. He looked amused, and a wide smile was about to curve itself onto his lips. If jumping after the phone wasn't a good idea, she didn't mind jumping down into Colton's arms instead. In the same moment her life was ending, she felt like a thirteen-year-old again. She felt like a fool. A lunatic. Like a girl so in need of love, she had put the world around her on silent mode.

Finally, Colton broke his gaze, and her hearing returned. It was as if someone had cut the invisible light that was connecting their gaze. Why in the world did he look away?

Iris's gaze broke to a girl screaming and wailing. Eventually, she understood, clapping her hands over her mouth. It was clear to her why Zoe looked so horrified and lost speech. The screaming belonged to the girl who'd just been chosen by the Beasts. Iris watched the girl throw herself in Colton's arms. The poor boy was in shock, clueless as she pounded her hands against his chest, cursing everyone in The Second.

Iris didn't know what to feel as Eva Washington was the one chosen as the Bride for the Beasts.

3

The girls watched Eva Washington plod to her death. She shuffled barefoot on the red carpet, hardly breathing against the fear inhabiting her lungs. The tensed muscles in her face wrinkled the features of her adolescent beauty. Iris watched the sticky tears in Eva's eyes thicken, and probably blur her destination to the Beasts' glowing spaceship.

Although the sun showed no empathy, still splaying its bright rays upon the scene, the Beasts' spaceship's unearthly light was even brighter. It had always been this way. Iris thought it was ironic how the Beasts hid behind the glaring light. Instead of wearing metal armors or using the latest hologram technologies, they hid behind a light brighter than the sun.

"Someone should help her," Iris mumbled, Zoe still standing next to her. "Eva's crying so hard, she can't see." Iris wasn't yet sure how to feel about having wished Eva taken by the Beasts just minutes ago. It wasn't like she had telepathic powers or something. This was beyond her perception, and she wasn't swooning about Colton being single now. In fact, Iris knew that from this moment on she'd have to live with some kind of unreasonable guilt about Eva for the rest of her life.

"My mother says that it's better to die before staring in the eyes of the Beast." Zoe commented, not taking her eyes off Eva.

"Has your mother ever been taken by a Beast?" Iris glared at her. Zoe shrugged so loud, Iris could hear her. She just wished people would stop commenting on and making things up about things they had no idea about. How would Zoe's mother have known anything about the

Beasts, when no one had ever seen one? In many ways, the Beasts were some kind of gods in The Second. People talked to them and they never talked back, yet they sent their orders to be followed somehow. Iris hated when elders told stories they couldn't back up with evidence.

An elder teacher standing nearby shushed Iris and Zoe with a tense finger on her pursed lips. Speak of the Devil, Iris thought, and shut up, staring at the ceremony.

None of the girls were allowed to talk in the Ceremony of the Beast. They stood on both sides of the red carpet leading to the ship, silently witnessing one of their own being sacrificed. The ceremony was a reminder for other girls, a torturing memory. Iris always wondered how the Beasts selected their Brides. Was it some kind of lottery? Did they follow a list with names? A prophecy maybe? Or did they choose the most beautiful? Iris was sure it wasn't the latter option. Last time, the girl wasn't as beautiful as Eva. Not even close. But who knew what beauty looked like in the eyes of the Beast?

Eva was walking toward the Beasts' ship. She wasn't permitted a stop of any kind. Every reluctant step Eva took closer, the girls on both sides did their best to silence their screams. Some of them wiped the trickling teardrops from their ripe cheeks. The punishment of sympathizing with the Bride was as horrible as Eva's inevitable fate. To the Beasts, this was a happy day. To be celebrated, and almost holy. Which led many to think the Beasts actually married the Brides. A disturbing suggestion, Iris had always thought.

A sudden cloud blocked the grinning sunlight, shading Eva's wedding dress with a gray stain. The girl chosen had to wear expensive, designer wedding dresses to meet the majestic Beasts. Just like any normal wedding, each girl wore their best make up and had their hair styled.

It was a painful process, being groomed while knowing one's horrible fate. No one could protest. It was the Law of the Beasts.

All girls were given a beautiful bouquet of roses, which were either synthetic or polyester, but smelled like real roses. For some reason, most things in The Second were artificial. The roses, as well as the grass in the local park, were as dead as the high metallic skyscrapers.

Eva wiped the tears from her eyes and began throwing random gazes toward the girls on both sides. This was the same girl who was probably going to be the Prom Queen, the same girl that everyone envied in school, Colton's girlfriend. Now her gaze was shattered, like splintered glass across the girls faces. She'd meet your eyes, but you'd think she wasn't even there. She'd become hollow, a fading portrait, soon to disappear in the Beasts' light. And it wasn't funny. Even though Eva hadn't been kind to the average girls like Iris and Zoe, none of the girls loved to see her as a Bride. Any of them could be in her shoes next week.

For a moment, Iris thought Eva was looking for Colton. Boys weren't supposed to stand in the front rows. Only the second and third. The ceremony was a girls' thing. There was nothing for the human boys to do here.

But each Bride had a father, a brother, or a boyfriend whose heart burned for her. But not even the strongest men in The Second defied the Beasts.

Empowered by delusional wishful thinking, Eva stole a last glance into her phone, which she had been holding with shivering hands. She looked like she wished it hadn't been her ID showing on the screen. It was clearly hers.

"How could you be so cruel to me?" she snapped, talking to the ship's blinding light, still walking forward. "I was about to go to college next year. I was going to be engaged to Colton Ray next month!"

A number of girls let out short sighs. This was news to everyone. So their relationship was serious. Iris could feel Zoe's blaming eyes on her skin.

"What?" Iris fisted an angry hand. She wasn't going to hit Zoe. She wanted to hit herself, for saying such a thing. The mere thought of her wish coming true was puzzling. "It's not like I'm a witch or something," she grumbled.

"We planned to get married while in college," Eva continued, shouting at the light. That silent light that told her what to do, but never talked back to her. "We've been planning to have two children; a boy named Jeremiah, and a girl named Flower."

Iris held a thin tear from being born in her eyes. No girl had talked to the Beasts this way before. Most of them sank to their knees, and pleaded that someone would help them and confront the Beasts. Some cried and fainted halfway through, until elders had to carry them as close as possible to the ship. And some prayed like in a chapel, brainwashed that this was their fate, and that they died as a sacrifice for the other girls to live--Iris wanted to kick-box those into the light.

But none of them had spoken in such an emotional way like Eva did. Her words reminded everyone that someone's life and dreams were being killed today. The problem was that most elders thought of the Call of the Beasts like natural disasters. Earthquakes, hurricanes, and volcanoes. Stuff like that happened all the time. And the Beasts, who ruled their world, must have a wisdom behind it.

Iris, unusually vulnerable, pulled out Zoe's phone and took another peek. The screen didn't show Eva's name.

The Beasts didn't believe in human names. It read: Beauty 57135LL; Eva's citizenship identification number in the United States of The Second.

The horn roared again, buzzing into each girl's bones. Instead of an answer to her question, the unseen Beasts were urging Eva to step closer toward her death. The silliest thought crossed Iris's mind. What if she just ran into the ship and at least peeked in, to see what they looked like? If they had the right to take one of them, didn't they have the right to know who they were?

Before disappearing into the light, Eva took one last glance at the girls. She waved a weakened goodbye as the girls lowered their chins to their chest and laced their hands together. It was as if Eva, the school's queen bee, had turned into a contagious epidemic they preferred to avoid. Many girls were teary-eyed though. But most of them were glad they hadn't been the one walking the red carpet.

Out of respect, Iris didn't lower her eyes. It was the least she could do. She was still fisting her hand, mad at herself for not standing up for Eva. It wasn't just the guilt moving her, but the fact that she could simply be next. Why wasn't anyone doing anything about it?

In an unexpected moment, Eva caught Iris's eyes, and nodded back, as if they had been lifelong friends and were now girl-coding each other. Iris glanced behind her for a second, not sure Eva meant her. Everyone else had their heads bowed to their chest. It was Iris Eva meant. Not only that. Eva mouthed something to Iris, something that gave her goosebumps on her skin, as Eva disappeared behind the light of the ship. Her darkest hour.

A second later, Iris caught sight of Colton standing second row on the other side. His blue eyes had turned into puddles of blurry tears. In front of him, girls raised their heads, most of them glad this was over. The ship's drone was deafening as it howled back up toward the sky.

Iris couldn't take her eyes off Colton, wondering if she should tell him what Eva mouthed to her. Who'd have thought that the queen bee, who treated her like shit, would ask this of her?

4

A week later, Iris sat in class, trying her best not to laugh at her history teacher, Mrs. Wormwood. When she wasn't able to contain herself, she had to pretend she was coughing, shielding her mouth with her hand.

"What's so funny?" Zoe whispered from the desk next to her. Sometimes Iris thought no one would have noticed all the crazy things she'd done if it weren't for her best friend following her like a shadow.

"Can't a girl even laugh without giving reasons in this school?" Iris sighed, not taking her eyes off of Mrs. Wormwood who, in spite of her old age, had fabulous pink hair like a twenty-year-old. It was a wig, which she would put on right before leaving her private office to go to the classroom. Iris had poured glue in the wig moments earlier, and wondered what Mrs. Wormwood's reaction would be once she realized she was stuck to her vice for life. She used a glue which was originally used to fix punctures in truck tires.

Iris straightened her back in her chair and mustered a serious face. It was a mystery to her why she pulled such pranks on her teachers. It just felt so revolutionarily good, as if her misbehavior was her camouflaged screaming at all elder people in The Second for not doing something about the Call of the Beast. In truth, almost everything in The Second bothered Iris. Now after Eva's mouthed words, it was harder to live in this place.

Iris focused her eyes on her teacher, pretending to be most attentive while her mind wandered away. It was a mind trick she'd learned lately to use with boring people everywhere. Instead of excusing herself or making faces, she'd stare at them while thinking about something else entirely. People, in general, never seemed to get it. All she had to do was nod at the end of the conversation, and wave goodbye. Surely it sometimes got her in trouble when someone was asking her to do something for them, but trouble should have been her middle name anyway.

At the moment, still pretending to be listening in class, her mind wandered to a place about the Beasts. She could not help wondering why the Beasts took the girls. And why only girls? Were the Beasts a male-only species? And what was their criteria in choosing the girls?

"Are you paying attention, Miss Beaumont?" her teacher snapped.

"I'm looking at you, aren't I, Mrs. Wormwood?" Iris flipped her mind's eye open, and came back to the real world.

"But you haven't answered my question," Mrs. Wormwood demanded, flipping back a strand of her hair.

"Oh," Iris shrugged. That was the trickiest part of her mind trick, when someone demanded an answer. What was she going to do now?

"So?" Mrs. Wormwood rose an eyebrow. Zoe was already mouthing the answer next to her, but Iris couldn't read her lips from her peripheral vision.

"Yes," Iris stood up and sighed, staring down at her fidgeting feet. It was the only word that popped up in her head. In a school that demanded students to strictly follow the rules, "yes" seemed like the easiest word to spit out. Iris thought it'd buy her time, until she could sneak a glance at Zoe's answer-mouthing lips.

Mrs. Wormwood's face had already reddened with anger. A bit over-reacting, Iris thought. What would she do when she discovered the wig problem? Last month, Mrs. Wormwood had sent Iris for four hours of psychiatry analysis due to her misbehavior. The month before, Iris had to write other students' essays as punishment for drawing what she thought the Beasts looked like on the margin of her exam paper. Two months prior to that, she had her phone confiscated for using it for unauthorized searches on the internet—she'd been searching the history of the civilization inhabiting the Earth before the Arrival of the Beasts. Stuff they weren't supposed to ask about in school.

Iris wondered what kind of punishment would be bestowed upon her once Mrs. Wormwood discovered the glued wig. But before that, she had to deal with not knowing the answer to some stupid question in her class.

"That's right," Mrs. Wormwood said, looking a bit confused. "You can sit down, Miss Beaumont," she said, giving her permission.

Iris tilted her head slightly, not getting it. She stared back at Zoe with inquisitive eyes. Zoe seemed happy her friend had finally paid attention in class.

"Sit down," Zoe whispered. "You got the right answer. Do you have a grounding wish, or what?"

Iris sat down with a crooked smile on her face. So the answer was simply a "yes?" Never mind what the question was, it was moments like these that proved her theory: that human beings were dumb and weak, and maybe, just maybe, they really deserved to be ruled by the Beasts.

5

"Are you attending Vera's birthday party on Saturday?" Zoe strode next to Iris in the hallway after class. She was clutching her books to her chest, trying to keep up with her pace. Iris always wondered why other girls plodded so lazily in school when there were like a million new things to explore in this world. Especially in a world as vague as theirs.

"No, I'm not," Iris hurried toward her locker. "I don't feel like it. It's the *same old, same old,* and I am fed up."

"How could you say that?" Zoe frowned. "Vera is going to be eighteen. That's every girl's best day of her life. It's rude not to share in the celebration."

"First of all, I think Vera is an airhead. Beautiful, but an airhead," Iris snapped her locker open. She did it with coolness and style, only to entertain herself. Boredom in The Second was just about the norm. She rummaged through and picked up some drawing tools, canvases, papers, and pencils. She was one of the rare people who still used a pencil, as they were only sold in auctions. "Second thing is, I don't understand all this celebrating being eighteen thing. It's a birthday, like any other."

"No, it isn't," Zoe's eyes followed the pencil in Iris's hand, as if she were embarrassed her friend still owned one. "Eighteen means you skipped the Call of the Beast. They only call seventeen-year-olds like you and me. You should be happy for Vera, and all eighteen-year-olds, for that matter."

Iris pulled out two small bottles filled with green liquid, and a strange device that looked like a metallic flashlight. She tucked both in her backpack. "Happy for her?" she slammed the locker shut. "Vera is arrogant and a bully, and everyone around her is a hypocrite because her father is a member of the Council. And what is the Council, Zoe? The elite humans who claim they communicate with the Beasts. The Beasts, Zoe. The ones who take one of us. Do you think I am supposed to celebrate my own eighteenth birthday and just be happy I escaped the Beasts' wrath? What about all those girls taken, Zoe?"

Zoe took a reluctant step away from Iris, whose voice had peaked enough for everyone around them to hear. She scanned the hallways with her eyes, worried that some teacher had heard Iris's rant. No one was supposed to insult the Beasts, or the Council.

"The Beasts must have a great wisdom for choosing the girls," Zoe said, straightening her back, and making sure others heard her clearly. Zoe always did her best to fit in. Iris didn't hate her for that. Zoe seemed like she couldn't deal with punishment and humiliation, like her. "My mother says the Beasts work in mysterious ways, and we shall not oppose them, for what they do, although seemingly harmful, is for the best of mankind."

"Crap." Iris grimaced, strapping her bag on her back. She was by no means affected by the students' piercing eyes. She'd been labeled an outcast long ago. "Do you even listen to yourself when you say this gibberish? Don't you really want to know the truth? Don't you wonder why the Beasts only take girls, never boys? Why seventeen? On what basis? And more curiously, don't you ever wonder what is done to those girls? Are they dead, humiliated, or what the heck is going on?"

"Enough! Miss Beaumont," Mrs. Wormwood appeared out of nowhere.

"But of course," Zoe lowered her head, answering on behalf of her friend. "She's very sorry."

Mrs. Wormwood took a moment, staring at Iris, who did her best not to laugh again. Seriously, she didn't want to miss the moment Mrs. Wormwood tried to pull off her wig.

"If you hadn't been grounded enough already, I would make you do more psychiatry hours," Mrs. Wormwood said. "But I am generous today. So, no more of that bad talking here. Understood?"

Iris nodded, partially to hide her smiling mouth. Mrs. Wormwood pulled her chin up and walked away.

"Look, I think it's better if we don't talk about this," Iris whispered to Zoe. "I just have all these questions in my head that no one wants to answer. And I can't help it. It's just me. I need to get answers."

"You should know that your questions are dangerous," Zoe lowered head. "Even the government doesn't ask such questions."

"Which is mind boggling, isn't it?" Iris let out a surrendering laugh. She'd decided her relationship with her best friend had come to a point where it was better to keep things shallow. It wasn't a bad thing. Her relationship with almost everyone else had come to this point. Either she talked about cute boys, birthdays and liked the same music everyone else liked, or she was considered weird.

All of this didn't matter, really. As long as Iris was capable of practicing her secret hobby, she was still happy. Now she had to go practice her secret. She patted Zoe on her shoulder and waved goodbye.

"Are you going where I think you're going?" Zoe asked helplessly.

Iris nodded, her thumbs tucked between her bag's straps and her shoulders.

"I assume I can't stop you," Zoe said.

Iris shook her head. She didn't like to talk about her secret hobby. It was a dangerous one, so she thought silence would help her skip the fear of doing it. "I have to go now," Iris turned around and walked away. It occurred to her that she hadn't practiced her secret hobby for three weeks. So why now?

Because of what Eva mouthed to me, she thought. That's why now!

A few steps farther, Zoe summoned Iris again.

"What now?" Iris puffed, and turned her head.

"Mrs. Wormwood's wig isn't going to be glued to her head by the way," Zoe said, waving the tube with the glue in the air. "I switched it so you only pasted some gel on her wig."

Iris narrowed her eyebrows. So her planned prank didn't work? Damn. But she couldn't be mad. Her friend had done this to save her from punishment. She did that a lot, and Iris loved her for that. Iris shook her head, flashing half a smile, and then turned around again and walked away.

"You're welcome." Zoe shouted in the back.

6

To practice her secret hobby, Iris had to sneak her way out of school, jumping over the electrocuting security fence guarded by two robot guards. Iris needed help so she had to call Cody Ray, Colton's nerdy younger brother, and total opposite. She'd met him sneaking out of school a day after Eva's Call. Cody was a year younger than Colton, a wannabe hacker, and the curious type. Like Iris, he wasn't content with The Second. The two outcasts clicked and became friends instantly. Zoe had accused Iris of only becoming friends with Cody as a stepping stone to his brother. Iris thought the idea was ridiculous, even though she still dreamt about that look she shared with Colton. In fact, Colton's eyes were Iris's only savior from Eva's mouthed words in her nightmares. The Beasts might have ruled her world, but never her dreams.

Cody was a 1st rate introvert. He was occasionally bullied--behind Colton's back of course. Colton, coming from a rich family, had never been the fighting type. He was good-looking, well-dressed, and too well-mannered to use his fists. No one was going to come near him anyways.

"Cody," Iris said firmly on the phone. She didn't want him to think she liked him. Nerdy boys fell in love like moths to a flame. Besides, she liked Colton. A lot.

"What's up, Beauty," he yawned.

"I told you not to call me Beauty," she snapped. She wore her hood of her jacket up over her head and stood behind the tree near the fence. She had about two minutes before the robot guards could locate her. The robots were changing shifts, and she only had a two-minute gap until the newer ones showed up. Cody had told her about this incredible loophole in the system--it had boggled her mind the first time she heard about it; why would robots change shifts? It wasn't like they got tired like humans. "Why aren't you in school, Cody?" she said.

"Because I'm in bed," he almost snored. "Sleeping my day away."

"That's ridiculous," Iris whispered, her eyes darting around. "I am all about skipping school. But if you sleep your day away, what will you do all night by yourself?"

"I love it when everyone else is asleep and I'm the only one awake. You know I'm not quite fond of people," Cody said. "Could you leave me be now. I was dreaming there was no one left in the world but me and the Beasts, and I was fighting them."

Iris smiled. The dude was definitely different, and interesting.

"I need your help, Cody. I have so little time," she said. "Get me out of school. Can you hack the fence's program, so I can climb it without frying like a stupid mosquito?"

"I know the hack, but I could go to jail for this," Cody's voice pitched. He wasn't going to sleep his day away anymore. "Why do you keep doing stuff like that?"

"Stuff like what?" Iris said nonchalantly. "I'm just ditching school. Now hurry, you lazy *beast*. The robots should appear any second."

"Alright, alright," Cody puffed. "You know why I'm helping you this time?"

Iris could hear him working his magic on his computer already. "Because I'm irresistible," she mocked him--and herself. "Now hurry. What's taking you so long?"

"No, dummy," he joked. "Because you don't care about being caught by the robot guards. If they catch you, you'll be punished, but it doesn't concern you a bit. All you worry about is not being able to do what you want to do. I like that."

"I like that too, actually," she considered, although she'd never analyzed it. She just did what she felt like doing, without worrying about what others thought of her.

"Here you go, Beauty," Cody said.

Iris heard him press the enter button on his computer. The fence's buzzing sound died. It was safe for her to climb up.

"But that's the last time I'll help you with this. If the Council finds out, me, and my family, will be toast."

"If you're so keen about your family, why are you hacking the system in the first place?" Iris growled, climbing the fence.

"I don't know why I do it, Iris. I just do."

"But I know why you do it," she thudded on the grass on the other side of the fence. "Because like me, you have questions. Only you don't care about the Beasts. You care about our history before the Beasts. You want to know how humanity ended up ruled by some aliens we call the Beasts, which can't even see. You want to know about what really happened to the The First United States."

"I'm going to buzz it back now," Cody said, neglecting her assumptions. She hated when he did that. Cody was the only one who shared her passion, but he was still conservative about it. It was like he had limits he wouldn't cross. And it was understandable, considering his family tree.

Iris heard the buzz return as the guards appeared behind the fence. Although they couldn't harm her, they were going to report her to the police who'd be looking for her soon.

"Thanks, Cody," she said. "I'll hang up now. I've got some running to do."

"Wait," Cody pleaded. "Where are you going?"

"I thought you wanted to sleep your day away."

"That was because it was going to be a boring day. You seem to have an adventure ahead," he said. "I'm curious about the reason you're escaping school. Where are you heading?"

"You won't like it."

"Oh," Cody said. Iris heard him shrug on the phone and the sound of him slumping in his chair. "To the Ruins?"

"Yes." There wasn't the slightest hint of hesitation in her voice. "And don't give me that crap about it being a forbidden place."

"I won't, Beauty," he said. "I'm just curious. You told me you haven't been there for about three months. Why now?"

"I guess I need something to distract me from thinking about Eva," she swallowed. "I believe the Ruins hold the answers to why the Beasts are doing this and who they are. I told you about it before. Remember?"

"You mean the Pentimento?" Cody sighed. The words sounded scary on his lips.

"Yes."

"The possible answer to how the world came to be messed up like this," he mumbled.

"I have to run now. Do you want to come?"

Cody didn't answer. Iris could hear him breathing heavily on the phone. Sometimes, she thought he was the kind of boy who loved to ask questions, but was afraid of knowing the answer.

"Cody?" Iris stopped in her tracks. It was as if Cody suddenly disappeared, without hanging up. "Come on, Cody," she insisted. "Don't waste my time. I don't like reluctant people. Either you want to risk coming with me to learn who the Beasts really are, or not."

"Is this Pentimento really the answer?" a voice asked in the phone. It was a calm voice, a bit shattered and worn out, but grounded. It was as if it belonged to someone strong and confident, but with a broken heart. It was Colton's voice.

Iris's eyes widened and her throat went dry once she recognized it. Was this what she'd hoped for, that her interaction with Cody would lead her to meet Colton? But wait. He wanted to come with her to practice the Pentimento? Why would he want to do this?

"Answer me," Colton demanded, then stopped for a moment. She heard him ask Cody what her name was. "Iris," he said. "Your name is Iris, right?"

"Yes." she said, hating how weakened she sounded all of a sudden.

"If I come with you to the Ruins, is it possible that I might learn what happened to Eva?" he said.

"I don't promise answers," she said. "But I'm sure it's a step closer to the truth."

"Wait up," Colton said without hesitation. "I'm coming to meet you."

7

"The Ruins are behind the Great Wall," Iris said to Colton, who was trying to catch up with her energetic walking. Iris preferred to have Colton behind her. She didn't want him to see it in her eyes how much she liked him. When he first arrived, he hadn't even remembered her. He hadn't remembered that most amazing moment of eye-locking before Eva's death. Iris thought it was natural. She was always kind of invisible to him, and who was she kidding? They had that moment right before his girlfriend received the Call to death. Nothing he would really want to remember.

"What?" Colton stopped. Iris had to turn around and face him. His black hair dangled down over his forehead, as he lowered his head down to talk to her.

"We don't really have the advantage to slow down," Iris said, taking a deep breath, and forgetting she was talking to Colton. "We shouldn't spend a lot of time in the Ruins, or the Slugs who live there could hurt us."

"Slugs?" he wondered.

Of course, Iris thought. Colton was no different from the other citizens who'd never heard about the Ruins, or the outlaws who lived in it.

"I don't care about any slugs, whoever they are," Colton followed.

"Then why do you look so confused?" She noticed the sparkling in his eyes had faded. Colton was grieving Eva's departure, but he was too proud to show it.

"You never told me the Ruins are behind the Great Wall. No one's supposed to go there." Colton remarked.

"Nothing of what we're about to do is going to be legal. It's one of the drawbacks of hanging out with me." Iris really wanted to make an impression, and she was filled with nerves about hanging out with him. But she wasn't going to change who she was for him. She wondered if it was even legal to have a crush on Colton while he was freshly mourning Eva.

"I haven't really thought about it," Colton said, a shade of sadness veiling his voice. This was a lesser Colton than the one her eyes had stalked all year long. "But I guess if the Ruins hold the secrets you're going to show me, it has to be behind the Great Wall. You're aware that this wall protects The Second from whatever danger lies outside, right?"

"It's also the only place that still has buildings made of brick, stone, and wood," Iris thought she'd pique his curiosity, "instead of this metallic world we live in."

"There are no buildings built of brick and wood anymore," Colton grimaced, lifting his head at the fortress of silver buildings behind them. She watched him take in her note, and see how dull the world around them looked. Shiny, but dull. "The Council has destroyed any of those ancient constructions built in The First United States."

"As long as you're with me, let's forget about anything they told you in school." Iris rather bragged. "I know you're used to believing the Council. It's time to open your eyes and realize we're living in a fortress prison called The *Second* United States. The Ruins are outer limits, and forbidden because they are the only place that has evidence of The First." Iris stepped closer, trying her best not to be affected by his manly scent. "There are *real* plants in the Ruins."

"That's impossible," Colton said. "The Earth's soil doesn't produce plants, nor crops. Thanks to the Council, they invented ways to grow crops in houses with no soil needed."

"You're still thinking of the Council." If she wasn't talking to Colton, she'd have pulled her hair and yelled. Funny how she couldn't tell someone she liked how stupid they were. "There are real buildings in the Ruins, and there are even real animals. I guess you'll have to see it yourself to believe it."

"Cody says you're smart," Colton rubbed his chin. She couldn't tell if Colton was impressed or annoyed with her. "Should I trust him?"

"Forget about Cody," she took another confident stride closer to him. "I'm Iris. I'm here in front of you. You shouldn't rely on anyone else's judgement. Either you're courageous enough to cross the line, or you're not."

"You're practically saying that crossing over to the Ruins, I might not come back." Colton said. A flick of admiration finally flashed in is eyes. Iris hoped she wasn't wrong about it. This was definitely admiration, right? And not because of my beauty, but because of me being just me.

"You want to know what happened to Eva or not?" she challenged him. "I've crossed before. About ten times so far. Can you?"

That flash of admiration sparkled again in his eyes. This time, he glanced at her from top to bottom. "How is it possible to even cross the Great Wall?" Colton said, looking over her shoulder at it. They were near enough to see the Great Wall in the distance; a construction disguised in some hologram technology, making it look like a sky in the distance, so it didn't hurt anyone's eyes or make citizens feel imprisoned from afar. In fact, the Great Wall had been everywhere in The Second all along. Whenever you saw a far away mirage you couldn't reach, it was nothing but the Great Wall. A deception to the eyes. The Council had their robot androids securing the Great Wall a mile ahead of it. They blocked anyone from passing through; protecting it, and protecting citizens from it. It was illegal to cross over under any circumstances. The robots had license to kill. Citizens of The Second had been obedient in general, except for a group who claimed they were the new revolution. They were always hunted down, only tens of them left scattered and uncaught--yet-- probably hiding in the Ruins.

"All we have to do is cross the guards," Iris smirked.

"And how are we going to do that?"

"We won't," Iris said. "There is a building at the corner of the street," she pointed at a bakery called the Barnum Bakery nearby. "The woman who owns it has a tunnel underneath that leads to the Ruins. Whenever you want to go there, you can use it. I'll introduce you."

"And why would that woman expose her life to such danger?" Colton asked.

"She is part of the revolution," Iris said.

"There is a revolution?"

"Of course there is," Iris sighed. Most people didn't know about it. "When society is full of nonsense like ours, when the government makes decisions people don't approve of and tells you that you have voted for those same decisions, sooner or later there will be a revolution."

"And I assume you're part of it," Colton said.

"Not at all." Iris laughed. "I'm just an ordinary girl who wants to know why she is subject to being taken by the Beasts. That's all. Once I know why and do something about it, I will sleep better at night. Maybe find a Prince Charming first, and then sleep better at night." She rolled her eyes. Part of it was at her attempt at flirting, and the other part, to cover up the fact that she actually was flirting with Colton.

"I'd like to know what happened to Eva, so I can sleep better at night too," Colton mumbled, staring at some invisible nowhere.

Iris squeezed his hand and shot him a sympathizing look. It was a true gesture. She might not have liked Eva, but she felt guilty about her being taken, after she had wished it herself. It was ironic that Colton and Iris were here together because of Eva.

Iris squeezed his hand again, and they began walking toward the bakery. His hand felt warm and strong, and so did her heart. She hadn't told him yet about Eva's words.

8

"What the heck is that?" Colton squinted at the shady Ruins.

Iris knew his infatuation with the tunnel and the Barnum Bakery hadn't withered yet, but the darkened Ruins beyond made his heart skip a beat. The sky above him was purplish, with a feeble sun trying to pass its orange hues through the thick layers of gray clouds. Hell, he doubted the sun was even there behind it. It was as if there was some kind of fire in the sky, one that had only been put out recently. All kinds of smoke swirled around them as they walked through the old and abandoned buildings. The Ruins smelled like ashes left in the rain.

"Welcome to the Ruins," Iris said. Her gaze was cautious and alert. She knew of the dangers lurking in every corner. She had never encountered a slug, a dangerous animal, or even a revolutionist. But she'd heard them so many times. There was always this feeling that she was being watched in here. That's why she preferred to go back before sunset, when the place dimmed from shades of gray to obscurely dark. "This is the world as it might have been before The Second. In your terms, this is probably The First."

"Do you really think this is the old world before the Beasts arrived?" Colton's mouth was left agape. He couldn't stop walking around and touching things, and taking pictures with his camera. Like Iris expected, whoever entered the Ruins was immediately entranced by the brick, stone, and wooden buildings.

"What else would it be?" Iris pulled him toward the building she wanted to go to. A place where she could practice the Pentimento.

"So the Beasts aren't the bad guys after all," Colton said. Iris shot him a worried look. "I mean, maybe the world was in *Ruins* and the Beasts saved us from it, like they always tell us in school. The Beasts designed a brand new place for us to live in, and we should be thankful."

"How could you say that?" Iris frowned.

"It's the most plausible explanation," Colton said. "Look at this horrible place."

A limping dog showed from behind a far wall. He looked thin and scruffy. Colton looked worried. She knew he'd never seen a real dog before. Dogs in The Second looked too good, with fair skin and hair. They didn't even drool, because they weren't real dogs. Only one of the Beasts' many inventions. You could even buy a dog that didn't bark or poop, if you so wished.

"It won't hurt you if you leave it be." Iris said.

"You've been bragging about this place having real animals. But they're deformed and ill. Look at him. I wouldn't want him in my world, and I should thank the Beasts for that. And you said you saw real plants? I bet they are as ugly as that." Colton pointed at a single green plant, barely making it out of the black soil covering the ground. It was full of fungus and weeds. "Is this the kind of plants you're talking about? And look at this soil. Would you eat something grown in here?" he sighed, staring at the darkened sky again. "What have our ancestors done to this place?"

"I can't believe you're saying this," Iris protested. Colton wasn't on her same frequency by any means. "If the Beasts saved us from a great danger, then why didn't they fix the Ruins as well?"

"Maybe the whole world outside is the Ruins. It might have been too big for them to fix, so they just picked a smaller place for us to live."

"Listen to yourself," Iris said, nearing the building she was heading to, Colton following her. "You don't make any sense."

"Maybe there is a great danger in the Ruins that could hurt us, or hurt the Beasts," Colton stopped and glared at her. He could feel the presence of unseen things here, although he couldn't hear or see them. "Maybe the Ruins is home to the Beasts' enemy."

"We don't have proof of any of that, and it will take us forever to keep guessing," Iris said. "All these theories come down to one last mind-boggling question: why do they take a girl every now and then?"

Colton's face knotted, remembering Eva again. Iris thought he was just confused; happy with his life in The Second, a popular and loved teen. His mind was pre-programmed by society's standards, and it wasn't really his fault. Thus, he was repeatedly trying to find excuses for the Beasts, so his life would make sense.

"If we want to know the truth about the Beasts, I have a better way. Come with me." Iris ushered him through the old buildings. Most of them were missing walls, and the buildings with brick walls were missing windows and doors. Blocks of cement and logs of wood scattered all around the streets, and the asphalt was mostly cracked and spilt into huge holes in places. Iris thought Colton should have appreciated her knowing her way around here, or he'd get lost or fall into some ditch.

"I admire you for coming here on your own," he said as they walked, a little calmer now, probably trying to reason things. "I'm still wondering though what this Pentimento thing is, and how it could help me learn about the Beasts."

Iris finally stopped in front of a six-story building, mostly in a much better condition than the rest. Although damaged, the building looked like a construction site with ladders, ropes, and all kinds of machinery—mostly made of wood—gathered around it. Someone had built some kind of wooden steps that grew tangent to the building's surface, like ladders spread diagonally to the left and to the right. It looked like a zigzag of wood on the walls from afar.

"Who did this?" Colton raised his head.

"Who else? I did it."

"You?" Colton grinned, that curve of admiration loping on his lips again.

Iris nodded proudly. "My father taught me."

"Your father knows about carpentry in a city made of steel and holograms?"

"A rare hobby, I know. He had been taught by his ancestors," Iris said. "I prefer you don't tell anyone. The Council get suspicious about anything unordinary."

"Being with you is illegal already," Colton smirked. He meant it with a good heart. "I've got blood on my hands already, and I'm not telling anyone anything. But Cody told me your father's hobby was painting."

"Cody told you a lot in such a short time," Iris said. "True, my father was some kind of painter in his youth."

Colton still looked dazzled by the construction. "So why did you go through all the hassle to build this stuff? Why in here, and why is this building so important?"

"Well," Iris sighed a little longer than usual. "My father never painted with a brush and then sold his glamour portraits for money. He practiced a forgotten art that had to do a lot with painting, though."

"And it has to do something with this building?" Colton inspected the building again, noticing the fading paint on its wall.

"Yes." Iris said, clasping her hands. As much as she liked Colton, telling him about her deepest passion was a tricky moment for her. What if he didn't like her hobby? That would have spoiled any future plans between them-- although she believed she'd never see him again after today anyway. But Iris, being who she was, couldn't stop thinking about it. Her passion for her art seemed to have overruled any relationships in her life. If she'd break up with a boyfriend, she'd survive. But if her passion was taken away from her, she would have died. "This building has a lot to do with my father's painting hobby."

"Wow. I am curious," Colton said. "What is this art and what is it called?"

Iris noticed that some of the sparkling in his eyes had returned now, and she was happy about it.

"Come on, tell me. I'm curious," Colton demanded.

"It's called Pentimento, and it's kind of forbidden by the Beasts. It's a beautiful, but dangerous art." Iris said, remembering the first time her father told her about what Pentimento was, and how it had changed her life and the way she thought about the Beasts forever.

9

When Iris was about five, a long time before her mother died, her father used to lock himself in the basement for hours while her mother braided her hair in front of the mirror. Iris wasn't blessed with good hair. It was naturally a bit stiff and hard to comb, blonde but not golden. Golden was always adored in The Second. Her hair grew much better in her adolescent years, if they had only waited and seen what this girl could do when she grew older. Her mother thought braiding Iris's hair camouflaged its defect, and made her daughter look stylish. Iris didn't care about her hair. If the world didn't like it, they'd better just look away. What piqued her curiosity was what her father was doing downstairs.

She might not have been that interested if everyone in the house hadn't been so secretive about it. Whatever Charles Beaumont was doing would be a great threat if the Beasts had known about it.

Iris had seen her mother fight with her father about the matter before. She'd be protesting that this hobby of his was going to expose them to the Council's wrath. Thus, the Beasts'.

"It's the only thing that makes me happy," Charles used to tell her mother. "And no one will ever know about it. My father did it and my grandfather did it. It runs in the family. I don't care if the damn Beasts don't allow it."

"No one said they didn't allow it," her mother had explained. "I don't think anyone even knows about this Pentimento. I just have a feeling that it breaks the Beasts' first, and only, commandment."

"I know what the first and only commandment is, mother," Iris had tiptoed in and raised her hand, as if she were in class. "Can I recite it?"

"And here we go with the Beasts' bloody commandment," Charles rolled his hands, and his eyes. "How can they teach this to the kids in school?"

"I'm in kindergarten, daddy," Iris had felt obliged to correct him. "Will go to school next year."

Iris's mother had shot Charles a look of guilt, then knelt down and held her daughter gently by her arms. "Please do tell your father what you have learned, Iris."

"The first commandant is," Iris straightened her back and made sure her top button was closed, then coughed to clear her voice. "'Thou shall not question the Beasts.'"

"Good girl," her mother rubbed her daughter's hair gently, avoiding Charles protesting eyes.

"In The Second we can live in prosperity and enjoy our lives under the sovereign of the Beasts. We are a nation of freedom, like no other," Iris saluted her mother like soldiers do. "Every individual is free to think and do what he pleases, as long as they abide by the law," she turned to her dad and rose a warning forefinger. "Never question the Beasts."

Charles sighed and ruffled her hair, as he had no choice to object. "How do they teach this to kids?" he mumbled, and climbed down the stairs to his double door basement.

"Don't be long," her mother had told Charles, then turned back to Iris. "And because you've been a good girl, I'll now comb your hair, then braid it the way you like it."

But then, Iris's mother got a call while doing her hair. Iris couldn't resist the curiosity of climbing down to the basement. To her surprise, her father had kept the door open.

Iris tiptoed into the room. It was full of books and paintings of all kinds. She wondered why her father still had some paper-books, when nobody used them anymore because they were available digitally everywhere.

Still, there was no straight law against owning old books just because no one liked them. Paper notebooks and pencils were still sold in auctions, as they were considered antiques. Painters used them mostly as part of their artistic endeavors, which were too expensive for them and made art a rare practice.

Painter! Iris thought. Her father must have been a painter of some sort. But why was he secretive about it?

Iris snuck closer to see what her father was doing. He was wearing his thick glasses while bowing over a painting she'd never seen before. It was of a woman with an unusual smile. A very serene smile, Iris thought. The woman in the painting wore a black veil, and the painting was mostly of dark and yellowed colors. Iris's father had tapped a sticker on its upper right. It was labeled, "Renaissance." Iris had no idea what that meant.

It didn't matter though. What Iris was interested in was the woman's amazing smile. She noticed that however she changed her angle looking at the smiling woman, the woman still smiled back at her, as if standing right in front of her.

Charles also had a stack of different oils and brushes next to him, a small and round magnifier, and what seemed like a metallic torch, like the one she later kept in her locker at school. Charles wasn't painting, but rather scratching the surface of the painting. Slightly. Carefully. Tentatively. And with love.

The painting seemed to be worth something that money couldn't buy, an expression she had heard her father say to describe her when he was in a good mood, smoking his cigar and rocking on his favorite chair.

Iris took a step closer and craned her head to take a better look. Her father was pouring a few drops of a strange green liquid from a thin bottle on the painting, before scratching again. He waited for a moment, then breathed onto the painting's surface, as if cooling it. Lastly, he used the magnifier to inspect the drawing.

Iris watched him let out a defeated sigh. He wasn't impressed with the results — with whatever it was that he'd expected to happen to the painting after pouring the liquid on it. He took his glass off and leaned back, then stretched his neck. Iris had no time to retreat. As he craned his neck, Charles caught a glimpse of her.

"Iris?" he said with a welcoming tone.

"I-I'm sorry," she took a step back. "I found the door open."

"You aren't supposed to climb down here," his face knotted, as he looked over her shoulder and back to her again. "How did you come down here? Where's your mother?" he whispered.

Iris's eyes widened, trying to match her father's conspiracy-minded mood. "She's on the phone," she whispered like Charles, not a pitch higher or lower. In fact, she tried to sound like him, which was too hard for her because he smoked, and his chest was full of garbage, like her mother used to say. Garbage in the chest thickened the voice.

"Do you think she will finish her call soon?" Charles raised an eyebrow, still worried her mother would come down and turn this into a dramatic soap opera.

"No," Iris giggled. "She's talking to auntie, so the conversation might take until dinner."

"Good," Charles nodded. "Come closer. Let me show you my secret."

"Really?" Iris jumped in place.

"Shhh," Charles flung a warning finger. "Don't raise your voice, and no matter what I show you, you have to promise me you won't tell anyone."

Iris nodded with a serious face.

"Not anyone," he insisted. "Now come here."

Iris approached the painting. The woman's smile was still marvelous when she got closer. "Who is she, daddy?"

"No one really knows," Charles sat Iris on his knees as he stared at the painting. "The painting is called the Mona Lisa though."

"What a beautiful name," Iris considered. "Can I have a name like that?"

Charles laughed. "You already have a better name. Iris." He looked into her eyes. Iris knew what her name meant. She'd always thought she was special in her parents' eyes, and therefore the name came up.

"Did you paint this woman?" Iris wondered.

"I wish I had," Charles chuckled. "I can't paint. Someone drew it a long, long time ago."

"How long?"

"I don't really know how long," Charles said. "But this painting has survived all the way since the ancients."

"Wow. The people who lived here before the Beasts arrived?"

"Like I said, no one can know about this," Charles said. "The Beasts don't like anyone asking too much about the past."

"And what were you doing with that liquid?" Iris reached for one of the bottles, but her father stopped her gently, cupping her hand into his palm.

"I was practicing a hobby of mine," he said, as he put her down. "It's called Pentimento."

"Penti-?" Iris looked puzzled by the word.

"-mento. It's not purely an American name. It came from an old land called Italy, which we think drowned in the sea many, many years ago. Italy was famous for its notorious painters. Pentimento is a painters' term," he explained.

"What does it mean?" Iris couldn't have been any more curious.

"It's hard to explain, but let me show you," he said, and ushered her to another painting on another table in the basement. Iris's hand patted her chest unconsciously when her eyes came upon the painting. It was beautiful. Enchanting. A feeling like no other swiped over her soul when she saw it. She tilted her head up toward Charles, wondering if he'd realized how beautiful the painting was.

"Take a longer look," Charles patted her, kneeling next to her. "Take in the picture and set your mind free," he said.

Iris turned back, and allowed the oil painting to hypnotize her, wondering how old brushes and strokes could outlive the strongest of nations and still have such an impact on the observer.

The painting was of two lovers, holding hands and running side by side towards a fountain. The eagerness in their eyes was breathtaking. Iris could understand how important the fountain was for the two lovers. Love itself, as ambiguous as it had seemed to Iris before, was portrayed just perfectly. Iris might have been too young to understand it, but the emotions oozing out of the painting were unavoidable. The girl in the painting was a bit chubby with full cheeks, something the people in The Second weren't used to. Girls were taught from a young age that the slimmer, the better-looking. The boy was beautiful, and it was Iris's first time she could accurately match the word "beautiful" with a boy. The painting was actually much better than the Mona Lisa because it was Iris's first sight of lovers. She wondered if she'd ever find someone to hold hands with her like that. Someone who'd belong to her and she'd belong to him. Were they going to look as beautiful together?

"Where are they running to, daddy?" she said, feeling a little embarrassed, watching the painting in his presence. What if he realized how much she liked the sight of the boy?

"It's a fountain," Charles said. "The Fountain of Love." Iris shrugged, as if it could quench her thirst. Somehow, it could. For Iris realized in that moment that not all thirst was for water. "The painter is called Fragonard. Jen-honore Fragorand. So this is Fragonard's Fountain of Love. A painting that was worth a lot of money at some point."

"And now?"

"The Beasts have no interest in such art. They like everything metallic and dull, like you see all around you. They are not fond of oil, natural colors, and human art."

Iris turned back to the painting. Now that she had known the boy and girl were running toward the Fountain of Love, she felt something in her chest briefly, like a butterfly or something. It was tickly and a little uncomfortable, but she didn't mind it.

"So tell me, Iris. Do you *see* this painting?" Charles said.

It sounded like an awkward question, but Iris nodded. Of course, she *saw* it.

"Take a closer look, Iris," her father said. "And tell me what you really see."

"A beautiful boy and an even more beautiful girl holding hands and staring at the fountain in front of them," she began. "They seem so curious, but also so happy."

"So you're sure they are both staring at the fountain?"

"Of course I'm sure, daddy!"

"Very nice," he smirked. "Now look at this," he began pouring the liquid onto the painting. Iris was going to stop him, so he wouldn't destroy the painting. She couldn't out of respect. "When I use this liquid on the painting and then scratch a little, then use a couple of other chemical components, the drawing starts to fade a little."

Iris took one of her father's magnifiers and neared it to the painting. Her father's words were true. "Stop," she demanded finally, unable to hold back. "Why do you want to ruin this beautiful painting?"

Charles laughed. "Don't worry. I'm not doing it any harm. This liquid only peels off a very thin layer of the paint."

"How thin?"

"So thin, you could barely see the effect with a microscope," Charles said. "When you used the magnifier, you only thought you had seen it change because of the blurry liquid and your concern about the boy and the girl in the painting," he winked at her, as he began moving the painting to another table.

Iris's face reddened. She was still confused. "Then what's the point of all this liquid and scratching?" she asked.

"This is the point," he signaled for her to follow him, as he pulled the painting gently out of its frame and folded it over a box on a third table. He clicked a button nearby and the box shone with white light from underneath the painting. "Now look at the painting again." Charles said.

Iris craned her neck, inspecting the much brighter painting now. The light from underneath made all the colors glare and weakened their contrast. "Do we have to use the light?" she said, unhappy with how the painting looked.

"Of course, we do. Just look. What do you *see*?" he had that smirk on his face again.

Iris was about to rub her eyes to see more clearly, when the truth struck her like lightning. Her mouth stood open and she couldn't make a sound. Under this condition, she saw that the boy and girl weren't both looking at the fountain. In fact, the boy was looking at the girl. He was mesmerized by her beauty. Infatuated by her. The painter had captured all the emotions a boy could have for someone he'd loved with so much detail. It was an even better painting than what she'd seen before. Except that the boy wasn't as beautiful. The look in his eyes showed great passion, but he himself wasn't good-looking like she'd seen before. The boy was simply, a beast.

"Do you still think they both are looking at the fountain?" her father said in a voice that resonated with her long after that. It wasn't a question. It was a celebration of some kind of magic.

"But how is this possible?" Iris wondered. "I'm sure I saw them both stare at the fountain back there. Is this magic?"

"Do you believe in magic?" her father raised a single eyebrow.

"I'd like to, but they say it doesn't exist in school."

"How many times do I have to tell you to forget about what the Council and the Beasts teach you?" Charles rambled. "If you believe in magic, then there will be magic. Anyhow, here is why you saw the boy and the girl looking at each other before," he tilted the painting a little, so the light hit it from a different angle now.

That was the unforgettable moment when Iris saw what Pentimento really meant for the first time. And it forever changed the way she saw things. Iris saw there were two pictures on that painting. An older one, where the boy was a beast and looked at the girl, and a newer painted-over one, where they both looked in the same direction at the Fountain of Love. Without the light, her father's liquids, and the scratching, it couldn't have been possible to see the painting underneath the painting.

"It's incredible," Iris let out a tight shriek.

"The painter began the painting with the boy as a beast, and looking in the girl's direction, in the beginning," Charles explained, staring at the picture. "Then for some reason, as the painting progressed, he changed his mind and decided to draw it from another perspective."

"But why?" Iris wondered. "Why did he think of the boy as a beast in the beginning?"

"This one escapes me," Charles said. "Fragorand lived in The First, and possibly even before The First. He must have had a change of heart at some point."

"Do you think Fragonard knew how the Beasts looked?"

"I don't think so, because the Beasts hadn't arrived in his time."

"Maybe he was painting the future." Iris suggested.

Charles laughed. "That's far fetched, Iris. If that is true, then who is the girl with the boy?"

"I am so confused, daddy." Iris couldn't take her eyes off the painting. "But I have a question. Why not paint from scratch, instead of painting-over?"

"My guess is that because canvases, the material they painted on, were incredibly expensive back then. Painters were usually poor folks all over history. At least that's what my father told me." Charles pulled back the painting and walked to his main desk, where he'd left his glasses. "And before them, my great ancestors, whoever they were, said the same. I haven't met many people who knew much about Pentimento in my life."

"I think I believe your ancestors," Iris said. "It's the only thing that makes sense to me, especially if the painter could paint so good."

"There is one other interpretation though," Charles said reluctantly. Iris didn't say a word. She thought her father was going to say what was lurking in her curious mind. "Maybe the painter intended for this to be a hidden message, like you've been suggesting. Something he wanted to pass on, but had to be kept from certain folk too. I couldn't think of a smarter way to do it. You bury whatever you want to say underneath whatever you want people to think they see. How clever, to have a secret blurred in front of people's eyes."

"Especially if you wanted your secret to survive through history," Iris mumbled, and then looked around her in the basement, wondering if many things were just a cover for another truth buried behind them. That would have made the world a lot less boring. She could spend her days exploring and looking for those secrets underneath every wall and every painting. When she grew older, she learned that the same applied to the words people spoke. They'd say something when the truth--their Pentimento-- was something else entirely. "So are all these paintings full of hidden paintings like these? Are they all Pentimentos?" Iris said.

Charles smiled. It was a serene smile, as if he was having the kind of conversation with his daughter he wished he had with his wife many times before. "Not all of them. And what you saw isn't exactly called Pentimento, but a variation of it."

"I don't follow."

"Pentimento isn't usually when you just find an older painting underneath another," he explained further. "But when the newer painting fades due to natural aging from years passing by, giving way to the older one to surface on its own."

"Is that possible?" Iris suddenly noticed her father was actually much more fun than her mother.

"It happens every day," he said, then shrugged. "Everything ages and peels off its layers until its bones are finally exposed, even humans. And only then, when we're able to see through those recent layers, right down there in the bare heart and soul of things, do we see what whatever we're looking at was meant to be in the first place. We see the truth."

"The truth?" Iris held a finger to her lips. "Are you saying everything around us is a lie, daddy?"

Charles lowered his head for a moment, looking at his laced fingers. Iris had expected him to tell her, "No, Iris. Not everything around is a lie. Just some silly paintings we might come across every now and then."

But Charles didn't say any of that. He said nothing, and his silence was puzzling. Iris waited for him to answer her, but then her mother's voice came interrupting.

Charles raised his head and winked at his daughter to go upstairs for now. "We'll talk about this in more detail later," he bowed down and kissed her. "Now I have to put on my boxing gloves. Your mom probably knows you know about my secret, and we'll have a little 'conversation' about you."

Iris tried her best not to laugh. She loved her mother. But her dad was right, one had to wear those gloves sometimes, when negotiating with her. Iris stopped by the door though and turned around, although she could hear her mother's footsteps stomping angrily down to the basement.

"Is it necessary that one figures out the layers underneath, daddy?" she thought this was a much easier question for him to answer. And she needed an answer before her mother arrived. "I mean, does the truth matter so much?"

Charles smiled. "I think it does. So we might have a chance to know who we really are."

10

"Your dad is really something, Iris," Colton said, standing in front of the building in the Ruins. "How come he wasn't hired by the Council? Such mentalities should serve the nation, and not be buried in a basement."

"My father isn't buried," Iris protested. "He does what he likes, and doesn't care about the Council."

"I didn't mean it that way," Colton shrugged, the sadness still pulling on his face. "So tell me, what does this Pentimento thing have to do with this building?" his eyes inspected all the wooden ladders climbing diagonally on the surface of the walls.

"The building is a Pentimento," Iris sighed. "Don't you get it?"

"How can a building be a Pentimento?" Colton scanned the building with his eyes, in case he missed something. "It's not a painting."

"Actually many of the brick and stone buildings in the Ruins are," Iris explained, ushering him closer to the wall. "Look," she pointed at a certain post that was shoulder-high.

"It's a wall, Iris," Colton began losing his patience.

"Look closer."

In spite of how absurd it seemed, Colton stared through the smoke surrounding them, unable to see something special on the brick wall. Iris pulled out one of her weird instruments from her bag, the one that looked like a silver torch. She clicked a button on it, and a purple light spread out on the wall.

"Can you see what the wall really is now?" she said, remembering when her father told her the same thing about the painting years ago.

"Actually yes," Colton grimaced, as his face shone with curiosity. "It's sort of painted. What is this?" he snatched Iris's instrument and strode back about ten feet, splaying the light on the wall, taking in the bigger picture. "It's an advertisement," he declared. His sudden excitement drew a small smile on Iris's face. The sadness on *his* face disappeared momentarily. She was glad for him. "It's an advertisement about The Council's bank, offering a great loan to better your life. The same advertisement that fills the streets of The Second," he strode back and gazed at Iris. "Why is there such an advertisement painted on a wall in the Ruins?"

"I'm not sure," she said, happy with Colton's enthusiasm. "My guess is that people still used to live in the Ruins when the Council first ruled. Maybe this place was a beginning, just before they designed our land. But that's not the point."

"It isn't? You're such strange girl, Iris," Colton pursed his lips. "Then what is the point of this building, and the ladders you designed yourself? Seriously, I thought you were going to tell me something that will help me know what happened to Eva."

Iris shrugged. Had she overdone the suspense? Or was it her subconscious trying to spend as much time as possible with Colton? After all, he wasn't here for her. It was for Eva. She should have respected that. "Switch that purple light on again," she told him. "And point it at the wall."

Colton shot her a criticizing look, but complied reluctantly. He found the button and switched it on again, pointing it at the wall, which was suddenly flooded with a purple light. "Wow." he mumbled.

"It's called a black light," Iris said. "Do you see what this is all about now?"

Colton didn't *see* at first. Iris had noticed that human eyes usually resisted the Pentimento when they first looked at it. It wasn't disbelief or stubbornness. Simply the habit of seeing things a certain way and the inability to change perspectives, all at once. She watched Colton's confusion wither slowly from his face. It looked like he wanted to say something, but was speechless. His eyes widened. His *irises* widened. The black light showed the older drawings beneath; the drawings covered with the Council's advertisement. "It's a Pentimento," Colton said. For a boy with such a confident voice, he sounded weakened and shocked now. He even touched the wall's surface with the tips of his fingers, to make sure it wasn't an illusion.

Iris nodded proudly, just like her father did with her. "The Council's advertisement runs as high as the building itself, probably covering older writings..."

"Which probably belongs to whoever inhabited the Earth before the Beasts came. The First." Colton cut her off, kneeling in front of the building, as if it were a holy temple. This was what he was looking for. A lead, however thin, so he could learn about the Beasts and find out what they had done to his girlfriend. "I knew it," he snapped his fingers. "Those before us must have left a sign. I knew it!" Colton stood up and turned to face Iris. He shot her that damn look again. Her body felt the warmth of his eyes on her. "You're a genius, Iris," he held her by the shoulder. Iris freaked out. His touch and his looks implied he was going to do something crazy. He leaned his face closer and kissed her on the cheek. It was a clutchy kiss, as if kissing a soldier friend after winning the war. Nothing of what Iris had dreamed of. Still, his lips sent shivers through her spine.

Colton, confused by the awkward moment, turned around and ran up the diagonal ladders on the wall, pointing the black light at every part he came across on the wall. "So you've come here all this time without telling anyone?" he kept climbing. "How many hours did you work on this building? Did you use your father's liquids and methods to peel off the Council's advertisement? Are there other buildings? What do they say?"

"Yes. I do come alone here often," Iris said, understanding the many questions roaming in his mind like cockroaches. It happened to her many times. "Part of the Council's advertisement had peeled on its own due to aging, probably erosion factors, which means the building, and the Ruins, are substantially old. Natural Pentimento usually happens like that, due to nature and aging. My father's methods are a bit unorthodox."

"Which means this is what the world looked like before the Beasts came." Colton's enthusiasm peaked even more. But then he stopped atop the ladder suddenly, gazing into the grayed distance of the Ruins. "But what really happened here? What happened to the world before the Beasts came?"

"Maybe you were right about the Beasts saving us from our own doing," Iris said, although she never bought into the theory. She was open for suggestions though.

"I know that was my original theory," Colton said. "But I can't imagine humans did this," he stared up at the sky. "I mean, we couldn't have done that to the planet. Look at how we crave nature. How we wish there were real and healthy trees and flowers in The Second. We love this world. Something else happened here. Maybe the Beasts themselves did this; destroyed the world to rule it thereafter."

"Maybe they destroyed us and then felt guilty about it," Iris was just playing along, hoping the conversation might lead somewhere.

"I don't think the Beasts are capable of feeling guilt," Colton gazed down at Iris. "They took Eva."

"And many other girls." Iris reminded him.

"Yes," Colton felt ashamed. "You know, I feel horrible that I had never questioned the Call of the Beast until they took Eva. I mean horrible things could be happening around us, and we'd never care, as long as we think they won't happen to us. Then when a close one gets hurt, we suddenly realize we are so vulnerable and weak."

Wow. Iris wanted to run up the ladders and hug him now. It was childish, she knew. Absurd. And almost disrespectful to Eva. But when someone you like so irrationally adds some rational reason for liking them, that's when it really feels right. Iris didn't think Colton thought deeply about others. He may not have been that way all along, but now he cared. Iris liked people who cared.

"If we work as a team, we might find the truth," Iris said.

Colton gave her that damn stare again, as if he wanted to apologize for not meeting her before. "So why don't they mention such a place in our schoolbooks?" he changed the subject. "I'm smelling a great conspiracy here."

"If there is a conspiracy, then it's the Council who must know what happened to the world in the past."

"Tell me, Iris. How much did you peel off of this wall?"

"Not much," she said. "It's a tiring and slow process. The black light-or any X-ray instrument-only shows what has partially worn off, but never what's buried underneath. I only worked on places where I thought the words underneath seemed to make sense. If you notice, what lies beneath the Council's painting is tons of scribbling and older ads. Someone thought this wall was a great place to rant. There are parts full of weird graffiti too."

"I noticed," Colton focused the light on a part near him. "Co," he began reading a peeled part that caught his eyes. "Ca," he continued. "Co again, and then the Council's advertisement hasn't peeled off yet. What do you think that is? Some kind of message? Co-ca-co?"

"I'm suspecting the letter after it is an L, but I abandoned this part, because the word didn't make any sense to me," she said. "Co-ca-col. What could that be?"

"You're right. It's like gibberish, although someone took the time with the calligraphy of the words, making them look nice and unusually big. Maybe that was what the older government in the First United States called themselves. Cocacolton." He smirked, knowing it wasn't funny. Iris thought he was just trying to ease the tension. She'd never considered Colton funny. Hot boys usually weren't.

"That'd be silly," Iris joked. "It also isn't what I am looking for."

Colton stopped on the ladder and pointed the light down at her. "I understand. We should be looking for something that could tell us about what happened, or what the world was like before the Beasts."

"Someone must have left a clue that's hidden underneath the Council's advertisement."

"Are you saying the Council's advertisement was here to cover up the past? The history of the Earth?" Colton said. "But why didn't the Council just blow up the buildings?"

"I'm not saying this was done intentionally," Iris said. "My father told me it's a natural process through the years. Newer generations paint their graffiti and their advertisements on the older painting of generations before. Every generation marks their words on the walls of history. When time passes, the older painting sometimes shows through, like on this wall."

"But you couldn't have spent all this time and not found something interesting," Colton noted. "What was the spot you found and think means something that makes sense?"

"Actually, I did find one sentence. Come down here," Iris said, and Colton did. She took the black light from him, and pointed it at a part of the wall that was eye-level to them.

"What the freaky deaky holy mushrooms is that?" Colton squinted. Iris almost laughed. "Oh," he scratched his head. "It's something Cody likes to say. I figured if I am going to start investigating things, I'd say it." Colton escaped his embarrassment by staring back at the words on the wall.

The words showing from underneath looked like they had been written by hand. Probably with some spray. It was an incomplete sentence. A long one:

"Human always see what the ..."

Colton read it and stopped. The rest of the sentence was buried under a drawing of a huge green credit card, part of the Council's advertisement. Colton gazed back at Iris. "Why this sentence?"

"I don't know," Iris shrugged her shoulders. "It's just a feeling I have. I mean 'Humans Always See What The...' What? It's such a strange statement. I have this deep inner feeling that it means a lot."

"I have no idea," Colton tried to rub some dust off the sentence with the palm of his hand.

"'Humans Always See What The...' and then?" Iris repeated, thinking.

Colton scratched the back of his head and let out an awkward laugh. "I don't really know. But I know why the sentence in this Pentimento caught your attention."

Iris watched him in silence.

"This sentence feels like it has to do something with Pentimento," Colton explained. "The idea of Pentimento is that you can find an older image of something underneath the newer one. It has a lot to do with seeing, and so does this sentence."

"I think you're right," Iris said. "I might have overreacted to it. It could be nothing," Iris lay her back against the wall. "I'm sorry. I know you really want to know what happened to Eva."

"I do," Colton said. "But how about you? Why are you doing this?"

Iris tried to keep her mouth shut. She wasn't going to tell him that she'd wished for his girlfriend to be taken by the Beasts, even if it was just a slip of the tongue. "I don't know," she said. "I guess since I was exposed to the Pentimento idea, I always wished there was more to this life. Also, and this is something I don't think you could relate to, I always felt like a stranger in a strange land in this world."

"Who told you I don't feel that way?" Colton leaned forward and placed his palm on the wall, right next to her head. His gaze freaked her out again and again. He was too close this time. She hadn't thought he'd be. "I've always felt like a stranger in my own body. I mean, I am a product of what others think of me. Colton, the hunk. Loved by girls, expected to win at sports and dress so cool everyday.

Something here about you," he shrugged. "I mean about the Ruins," he switched his gaze to the wall. *Way to go, Colton, she thought. Comparing me to the Ruins.* "I know I hated it when I first stepped into it. But now I suddenly fell in love with the Ruins. With all the gray shades hovering above it, it feels likes a real place, where I could be who I want to be."

"So you're not disappointed I couldn't be of much help?" Iris wondered. Did this mean she could see him again?

"Are you kidding me," Colton took some steps back and raised his hands in the air. "With all those possible Pentimentos here, we'll keep on looking until we know what happened before the Beasts came..."

Suddenly, Iris could hear a faint low hum droning somewhere. She exchanged worried looks with Colton, hoping the slugs hadn't found them. But it wasn't the slugs. It was a faint sound coming from The Second itself.

"It's the horn," Colton said, his face tightening. "Why aren't our phones beeping?"

"There is no signal in the Ruins," Iris said, pulling his hands. "We have to go back now. It's only been a week since..." she couldn't say 'Eva.'

"We can't let this keep happening, Iris," Colton said. "I wonder which girl has been chosen this time."

11

Iris headed home later and ate dinner with her father, who still took care of her dead mother's vacant chair. Iris saw the placemat was there, and a fork and a spoon, and an empty plate. Her father wasn't crazy. He just did it out of respect to his deceased wife. Once in a while, Iris would catch him staring at the chair, wondering if her mother's ghost sat there with them.

Charles hadn't been as talkative since his wife died. He'd even abandoned his basement hobby since then, as if there was no point of searching for the truth, if he couldn't share it with the love of his life. Iris respected that and ate silently.

Unlike other families, Charles wasn't worried about his young girl turning seventeen. Parents in The Second spent an overly-anxious year when their daughters reached that age. Zoe's parents were like that. The fear for their child's safety oozed out of their eyes, thinking their daughter didn't notice it. "Being a teenager sucks," Zoe would say. No wonder she was so anxious to attend Vera's birthday when the girl only bullied her in school. Eighteen was like going to heaven, being freed from a death sentence, and even splitting up one's cocoon and finally becoming a butterfly.

But if families were that worried, they got to celebrate their child's freedom once every week. And today was such a day, because another girl had been chosen by the Beasts. One girl's misery was all other girls' happiness in The Second--and probably for at least five more days. A Call by the Beasts never came sooner than five days of the last summons.

"I escaped school today, daddy," Iris said, not looking at him.

"And why do you feel the need to tell me?" Charles breathed into the soup. He was neither angry nor happy. He was just there, unsure of what to feel about the world.

"Hmm...I just thought it'd be better coming from me, than from the school's principal."

"The school stopped informing me a while ago, since I never replied," he said.

Iris thought her father was the best in the world, although he seemed a bit irresponsible lately. She thought he didn't believe in the system, just like her, and so he preferred not to interact with it. To just be there, a clown in the circus.

"I know I am supposed to be happy that you're not yelling at me for skipping school like Zoe's parents," Iris said. "But sometimes I am afraid you've given up on me."

Charles dropped the spoon and faced her. He tried smiling in an assuring way, but it came out weak and fragile. "I will never give up on you," he cupped her hand into his. "I will fight dragons for you."

"Dragons aren't real, dad," she smiled. She loved how he still talked to her as if she were ten. Frankly, she missed the feeling of being ten, where mysteries and dangers were just happy imaginations filling her mind. Now, she was growing up in the real world, where everything was so real, it cut through the flesh sometimes.

"Then I'll fight the Beasts," he pulled his hand back and drank the soup straight from the bowl. "Sorry, Gabrielle," he nodded at her mother's chair. Her name was Gabrielle-Suzanne, and she would have never allowed it.

"Sorry mother," Iris followed, and drank straight from the bowl as well. Her father burped after. Iris sucked at burping. She couldn't do it.

"Now I can slay dragons and Beasts for you," he wiped his lips with the back of his hand. Iris laughed so hard, her stomach ached a bit.

"So what was her name?" Charles's face changed suddenly. Iris knew he was asking about the girl who'd been chosen today. Her mouth twitched, remembering the scene, watching her cry herself to death as she walked toward the ship of light.

"Elia Wilson," Iris said, lowering her head with respect. No family liked to talk about the Brides at dinner. No one even talked about the Brides after they were gone. Her name wasn't even going to be mentioned in the electronic paper's obituary the day after. Being the Bride was even worse than death itself. A member of society, a girl, has just vanished from The Second today. She hadn't even left any Pentimento behind. Her name would even disappear from records in the years to come. It was the Law of the Beast: We'll give you all you need to live the metallic dead life you've asked for, and we will take one girl full of life every now and then.

All Iris could think about now was Elia's family, sitting at some dinner table, asked to pretend their daughter never existed. It was against the law to protest, mourn, or even question. In fact, many people embraced the idea that the Call of the Beast was a savior for humanity. That one girl had to be sacrificed for some holy wisdom that made no sense. There was this old story that a woman prophet had descended upon Earth centuries ago, to show humans the right path. A woman who was believed to have been a descendent of the Beasts. But humanity, in its denial for all good sent to it, refused to believe in her and hung her on a cross to die. Unknown to them, the woman had been killed and elevated back up to the Beasts, to wash over the sins of humanity. And that's why the Beasts take a girl in their Call, as a remembrance for humanity's unkind actions of killing the lovely Lady Jesus. Theories and stories were a dime a dozen, the truth was the one story never told.

"Elia Wilson," Charles said the name as if reciting a prayer. He flipped his phone on, and looked up her name and address. "Got it." he said. "You want to do this?" He asked his daughter.

Iris nodded and wiped her mouth, then stood up. "Let's do it. Elia deserves to be remembered." Iris went back to her room and pulled a card box from under the bed. Inside the box, there was something special in a puddle of mud. It was something that none had seen in The Second before. Iris had found it in the Ruins, and taken good care of it ever since. Her father was calling her. It was time to do it.

12

Iris sat next to her father in their car parked in front of a metallic two-story house. It was snowing, and the house was almost dark, all but the dinning room on the first floor.

"Do you want me to do it like last time?" Charles asked.

"Last time it was Eva's house," Iris said. "I was afraid they wouldn't understand if they saw me. But I didn't know Elia Wilson. I hope they accept it. I won't let them see me anyways."

"Fine, then," Charles said, and turned his gaze back to the house. "You have it with you?"

"I do," Iris felt her coat's right pocket. Something fluffy was in there, wrapped in some sort of plastic. It was the precious thing she'd kept in the box under the bed. Iris didn't need to pull it out now. She opened the door and stepped into the thick snow, and walked towards the Wilson's front door.

Iris took one last glance back at her father in the car. Charles nodded with a weak smile. Iris turned back, holding her precious gift in her hands. A red rose. A real and rare one she'd found in the Ruins. Amidst all the grayness, a blood-red rose found alive. It was the only plant that grew healthy and undamaged in the Ruins. Iris never knew why.

The rose was carefully wrapped in a transparent foil. Iris knelt down and laid it on the snow before the door. She treated it with care, like a newborn baby.

Then she started carving some words with her gloved hands in the thick snow. She carved it while facing the car, her back to the door. She raised her thumbs in Charles's direction when she finished. She turned around and took a deep breath. Charles had already started the engine of his car by then.

Iris took another deep breath and rang the bell, then ran back to her car, almost stumbling in the snow. She opened the door as Charles pushed the gas pedal ahead, as if they both had just robbed a bank.

"Wait, dad," she pleaded, watching a woman open the door. It was probably Elia's mother. "I want to see."

Charles slowed the car down behind a fence so the mother wouldn't see them. And Iris *saw*.

The mother took a moment to register what she was holding in her hands, then slowly smiled at the beauty of the red rose. It didn't matter that she hadn't seen anything like it before. A rose was as beautiful as morning sunshine. You'd love it, even if you were dead.

Elia's mother unwrapped it and smelled it, staring at the stars in the sky above. She looked around for whoever sent this beautiful rose for the Wilsons, but couldn't see them.

"Look down at the snow," Iris whispered. "Please."

The woman finally caught the words engraved in the snow. Her hands shivered reading the words, the rose sliding through her hands, its petals scattering on the snow. The woman fell on her knees and started crying to the words Iris carved in the snow:

Elia Robert Wilson. You will always be remembered.

13

It wasn't easy for Colton to ask Eva's parents' permission to enter her room. They had only been together three months, and it wasn't like Eva had been his soul mate or anything. Both of them were lost souls in a high school that secretly demanded you acted like society expected you to. As son and daughter of elders who were part of the elite Council, Eva and Colton played their parts right, wishing it was only until they went to college. Then they'd get to be whoever they wanted to be, without all that pressure--at least Colton thought so. He wasn't sure about Eva, and it was one of the things that always threatened their relationship.

Eva's father permitted Colton the entry, although he demanded it to be quick. Colton said he only wanted to gather a present he had given her, so he could honor her memory. Remembering a Bride, although against the Law of the Beast, was a very intimate and special matter, practiced secretly among some citizens. It wasn't like the Beasts didn't know about it. They probably did. But the Beasts never showed their true evil nature, Colton was beginning to think. They were hiding somewhere up there in the sky, guarded by the lighting of their protective ships, playing The Second like marionettes. All under the name of democracy and the Law of the Beast. A few families secretly remembering the lost ones wasn't a big deal.

Colton entered Eva's room and locked the door behind him, leaving her mother crying somewhere in the kitchen. She didn't look like she could pretend her daughter didn't exist yet. After all, it had been more than a week and no one had emptied the room.

Eva's room was classy. Everything in it was too expensive and glaringly girly. Colton didn't know what to look for. After he had parted with Iris, he'd been wandering the streets like a lost beggar trying to find a place he could call home. Everything around him felt so fake after he'd been exposed to the Ruins and the idea of Pentimento. He'd started to question everything around him. And all of this was because of this unusual girl named Iris. Her name brought a smile to his face. He wasn't supposed to feel this way about anyone but Eva at the time. But he couldn't help it. He'd never missed a girl so fast. Hell, he'd only gotten to know her a little bit today, and they weren't even friends.

But Iris was irresistible. And the best part was she didn't know it. Colton thought he'd never really met a girl like her before. He thought Iris was average in the looks department. A face like so many other girls. A body that was okay. Nothing special about her in the shallow way men were expected to seek in girls in The Second. But her spirit was so sexy in the most unexplainable way.

Colton shook his head and sat on Eva's bed. This wasn't right. He'd never been interested in Eva the way he was in Iris, but Eva was still his ex, and no new girl was going to take her place unless he felt he did all he could to honor her somehow. Only, he didn't know how.

Why was he really in this room? Was he expecting to discover something? Eva was an open book. She wasn't interested in the unknown. She'd even said she approved of the Beasts' laws. Somehow, she was confident she'd never be chosen as a Bride because she was a Council member's daughter.

"You were so wrong, Eva," Colton buried his head in his hands. "If even the Council's daughters aren't immune, then who is? Do the Beasts have some criteria in choosing the girls? If so, why did they choose you, Eva?"

Colton inhaled all the air he could before his confusion suffocated him. The only thing that brought a smile to his face was Iris again.

Gosh, who is this girl? I haven't even kissed her.

Colton stood up and began rummaging through Eva's stuff. It seemed like a dull task now. He almost knew everything about Eva. She loved to take photos of herself, and always had to be positioned in the front of any photo taken of her with anyone else. Colton remembered that she didn't like to be photographed next to girls who matched her beauty. There was a substantial number of photos of them together as well. Always hugging him, clinging to him, and making sure she was up front in those pictures as well. Colton thought he looked stiff in the pictures. "What a jerk," he called himself. He thought his poses were snotty and unnatural. "Oh. Come on. You couldn't have changed so fast," he talked to his reflection in Eva's wall mirror. "This one in the pictures is you. Always has been. You weren't the kindest of students, and if Cody hadn't told you about this curious girl who had a clue about the Beasts, you'd never have even looked at Iris. Don't try to play as if you had a change of heart."

Colton began to worry. Talking to himself wasn't something he usually did. Besides, he remembered now when he first saw Iris dangling her feet from above the principal's office. He thought she had big toes at first. Something he hated in girls. But then when he stared at that clumsy girl with chocolate smearing her lower lip, something happened to him. Something he could not explain. He doubted she had any idea he was looking up to yell at her, since her chocolate wrapper fell right on his face. It wasn't the phone that caught his attention the first time.

What's wrong with me? I couldn't even open my mouth and shout at her when I saw her staring at me as if I was the Easter Bunny.

Colton ruffled his hair and shook Iris away from his brain, although she had already booked a place somewhere inside his skull.

He was about to put Eva's album back in the drawer, when he saw a photo standing next to Vera. They were close and almost had the same taste. That's why they rarely took pictures together. Each one was intimidated by the other's beauty. Colton knew tomorrow was Vera's birthday--he'd been invited before Eva was taken. He contemplated going or not. An eighteenth birthday for a girl in The Second was a big deal, and he respected that.

Colton flipped through one more pictures before a vision struck him. A vision that urged him to flip back to Eva's picture with Vera. A third girl was standing next to them. Someone he knew.

Colton looked more closely at the picture. The three girls were embracing in the school's stadium, probably before one of his Steelball games, which he was a master at. He was right. He knew the third girl. Next to Vera and Eva, stood Elia Wilson. She was a fascinating beauty like the other two.

14

While waiting for Zoe the next day, Iris didn't finish her homework--she thought she was too old for calling it homework anyway. She spent her time surfing the internet instead, looking for answers about the Brides. Why were these girls really taken? What did the Beasts do to them, and on what basis were they chosen?

As usual, no one discussed the subject freely. Not on the social networks, not in private forums, and not even in private messages between friends. The Call of the Beast had been happening for decades. It was unquestionable, and no one longed for explanation anymore. No one was ever blamed for these kind of catastrophes. And it always boggled her mind.

Still, she wasn't going to give up. Someone, somewhere, knew something about the Beasts. If they were communicating with the Council, teaching them what to tell us, then there must be someone who had seen or talked to a Beast face to face somehow.

Iris estimated thousands of girls had been taken throughout the years. The Beasts took about fifty-two Brides a year. More or less. They'd never been specific about dates. The big problem for Iris was that the Brides' names were erased from existence, even their family pretended they had never been born--at least they were forced to. This left no traces for Iris to find enough connections between the girls. She could only track the ones who'd been taken since she was fifteen, the first time she'd asked her father to place a rose in front of the girls' houses and let their parents know they'd be remembered. She'd found the roses in the Ruins and thought they would leave a precious impression if given to the parents.

Suddenly, her room's door sprang open and Zoe dashed in.

"Zoe!" Iris said. "You look fantastic."

"Really?" Zoe said. She was dressed very girly in a blue dress with an extra embroidered shawl. She even had a blue ribbon in her hair. "It's going to be a big birthday, you know. I thought I'd do my best to look as good as them."

"Come here, sweetie," Iris pulled her closer, and fluffed Zoe's hair a bit. "You look like you're going to meet Prince Charming today."

"Yeah," Zoe rolled her eyes. "As if there is one for me."

"Don't say that," Iris said, Colton's image flashing in her head. "He is waiting for you. It's just that you're too busy with all the boys chasing you, so he's gotta wait." They both snickered.

"So no homework, I guess," Iris said.

"Don't let my appearance fool you," Zoe flashed two notebooks from under her dress. "I finished mine and yours, so you could rest your case."

"Oh, Zoe. You're amazing." Iris hugged her. "But you didn't really have to do mine."

"I had free time, and know you hardly pay attention in class. I want you to have good grades to go to college."

Iris hugged her again. It wasn't for the homework. She didn't really like someone doing hers. It was because of Zoe's unconditional love for her.

"Easy with the dress," Zoe pretended to be snotty. "You're going to mess it up."

"Ah," Iris placed a hand on her mouth. "I'm really sorry, my princess."

"I have about half an hour with you, before Cody picks me up." Zoe said.

"What? Cody?" Iris's eyes shimmered. How didn't she think of matching them up before? She thought they'd make a good couple.

"He called me and told me he got my phone number by hacking yours," Zoe explained. "I think he didn't realize that was a creepy thing to do. He thought it'd make me like him, so he could ask me to go with him to Vera's birthday."

"That's something that Cody would do," Iris pouted. "Sorry for that. I guess he liked you and didn't know how to tell you." Iris wasn't going to tell her that Cody liked her too. She thought Zoe should have a chance with him, and then decide if she liked him or not.

"Actually, I thought I'd go with someone you know, instead of feeling so alienated at Vera's birthday."

"You're the one who wants to go," Iris pursed her lips.

"It's just a birthday. And I'd like to see how girls celebrate when they're eighteen."

"If you say so."

"So tell me, how many rules have you broken since you left school this morning?"

"A lot," Iris said.

"Oh, so skipping school while sticking your tongue out to a robot wasn't enough?" Zoe sat on the bed, imitating how princesses lifted their dresses before sitting.

"Thanks for switching the glue by the way," Iris laughed.

"I am still waiting for a thank you from Mrs. Wormwood, but I guess that will never happen, since she would have to know what was going to happen to her first, in order to thank me," Zoe said. "I'm a saint. Ain't I?"

"You are. Aren't you going to ask me again what other rules I broke today?"

"I can guess," Zoe tilted her head. "You went to the Ruins, practiced that weird hobby of yours. Found out nothing about the Beasts, and came back home. You're very predictable." she joked.

"And who did I go to the Ruins with?" Iris grinned.

"Cody?" Zoe guessed.

Iris shook her head "no," and bit her lip.

"I'm not sure why you're biting your lip. You know you can't keep a secret from me anyway."

"Colton."

"Colton who?" Zoe said.

"Colton." Iris stressed.

"The Colton?" Zoe's eyes almost popped out of her head.

Iris nodded with a grin on her face. "He is Cody's brother. When he heard I knew something about the Beasts in the Ruins, he offered to come."

Iris recited all that happened between her and Colton to Zoe, who'd been so excited, she thought she'd skip the birthday. But then Cody called and said he'd be late another half an hour.

Having gossiped all they could about Colton, Zoe couldn't resist asking Iris about what she'd been searching the internet for.

"Did you ever wonder what the Beasts really look like, Zoe?" she tried to sound uninterested, as if she were just making conversation until Cody arrived.

"Will you ever stop being curious about them?" Zoe fidgeted, looking uncomfortable in her high heels.

"Are you saying you're not curious yourself?" Iris's stare was sharp, piercing through whatever fake disinterest Zoe showed. Iris was sure she was curious.

"I am," Zoe avoided her friend's eyes. "But thou shall not question the Beast." she craned her head, as if someone could have heard them.

"We're not questioning them. We're having a conversation about them. Don't be such a coward." Iris said.

"Alright," Zoe took off the high heels until Cody arrived. "I guess I broke all the rules today, wearing such a dress, and going out with a boy I barely know. So here is what I hear. Some students say the Beasts look like Aliens."

"Aliens?"

"Those green creatures who look like frogs and have antennas in their heads?" Zoe reminded her.

"I know what aliens are," Iris mocked her back. "But how do aliens really look? I mean all that green stuff about them was only made to entertain kids. Besides, we all know that the Beasts are the aliens, whatever they look like."

"Don't shoot the messenger. I am just telling you what I heard."

"I don't care about what you heard, Zoe. Use your head. Tell me what you *think*."

"You want my opinion?" Zoe raised her eyebrows. "You usually never listen to anything I say. Anyways, I think they are far more advanced than us. I mean, whatever metallic technology we live in with all those hologram inventions and communication methods, they live a much more transcendent life, if I may suggest."

"Like how?"

"I don't know," Zoe shook her shoulders again. "I can't imagine what I haven't seen. It's just pure logic. If they are our rulers whom we never see, and all of us are obeying them, even the Council, then those Beasts are the shit." Zoe clapped her mouth with her hand instantly.

"Lady Jesus, see what talking with you made me do? I have never said the S word before."

"Lady Jesus?" Iris neglected Zoe's silly concern for uttering bad words. "You don't believe in that crap."

"Oh, so this night is going to be full of crap and shit," Zoe said. "My mom believes in it. I don't know what to believe. I am just not as sophisticated as you. Since when do we have such deep conversations? Our friendship is built on you being the outcast who asks questions, and me being the shallow girl who saves your ass."

"You said ass," Iris laughed.

"Well, the train has run off the rails tonight," Zoe said. "And it's all because of you and your never-ending questions."

"Do you ever wonder why the Beasts take only girls?" Iris wondered. "And don't say it's all about Lady Jesus again."

"Don't worry. I won't. I even heard that Jesus is a man's name," Zoe said. "To tell you the truth, your question is the one that I keep asking myself all the time."

"So you ask questions." Iris pointed out.

"Of course I ask, Iris. I just don't utter them, so I won't get expelled or hurt. I have to work hard to earn a place in college and have a life. But when I lay alone in bed and I'm just about to go to sleep every night, I ask myself why the Beasts only take girls."

"And?"

"Maybe they are only a male species," Zoe suggested. "Or at least some weird sexless species. Maybe with all the power they have, they have that weakness that they can't breed. And in some twist of life, they need females from The Second to breed."

"It's a plausible suggestion," Iris considered. "You think that's why they saved the planet from decaying, to preserve the female baby-makers?"

"Could be. But then a million doors to other questions will open."

"Like?"

"Like what do their babies look like?" Zoe said. "Part human, part Beast?"

"We don't even know what the Beasts look like, so it's unimaginable."

"And what kind of species are they?" Zoe seemed to like the conversation now. "Are the babies also Beasts, or some second generation creatures? If so, where are they, or shouldn't we see them too?"

"Then how do you think they choose the girls?" Iris asked. "According to you, they have to be the most fertile."

"Or beautiful, in case the Beasts are really ugly. They call the girls Brides, right? This sounds like a marriage to me."

"That's a bit inaccurate," Iris corrected. "We are the ones who called them Brides and Beasts. And it stuck since then. The Beasts never called themselves anything."

"They could have easily called themselves gods if you ask me," Zoe said.

"So you really think they choose beautiful girls? Because I went over it in my head today and I noticed not all the girls were airheads." Iris said.

"Before we even continue this conversation, you need to change your mind about all beautiful girls being airheads. That just isn't true."

"I didn't say that," Iris said. "But most of them are."

"No, that's not true either," Zoe insisted. "Elia Wilson for instance, was so close to being the youngest tennis player in The Second. Two years from now she'd have been winning trophies, and she was a ten in the book of beauties."

"She was?" Iris had never told Zoe about the roses she and her dad left at girls' doors.

"See? And many other Brides have been very interesting girls. Besides, I did some research," Zoe said. "Absolute beauty was never the main criteria in choosing."

"Research?" Iris almost jumped from her chair. "So you do research and never tell me?"

"I can't tell you, Iris," Zoe said. "You'd keep talking about it all the time. And I want to talk about life, cute boys, and things that matter at my age. Anyhow, now you know, and you'll never stop talking about it."

"So if not beauty, then what?" Iris was back to the point again.

"I really don't know," Zoe said. "All I can think of is that the girls have something precious to the Beasts. Something so subtle, none of us can pick it out so easily, unless we've befriended all the girls before they were taken."

"Which is just impossible," Iris said. "You know what new question just popped in my head?"

"Enlighten me," Zoe pursed her lips.

"What if there is something the Beasts are looking for in those girls, and once they find it, collect it, accumulate it or whatever, they have no more need for The Second?"

Zoe shrugged. "You mean..."

"I mean that once they take what they want, we will not be of use to them anymore," Iris said. "What if they never saved us? What if they only preserved us, like some lab rats and then," Iris puffed air from the palm of her hands. "Poof."

"That's some creepy thought," Zoe said. "I don't want to even consider it."

The silence stole the air from the room for a moment as Iris, like usual, never looked away from Zoe, convinced her conclusion was most plausible. Her stare was too sharp. Zoe didn't know what to do, until a small pebble came knocking on Iris's window.

"Who could that be?" Iris wondered, walking to the window.

"It's probably Cody," Zoe said. "Maybe he is embarrassed to knock."

"Why would he be embarrassed?" Iris pulled the window open, as another pebble hit her in the forehead. She took the hit like a champ, then looked down with anger in her eyes.

"Sorry," said the voice from below. Iris couldn't believe her eyes. It was Colton.

15

"What are you doing here?" Iris asked, half-blushing. Colton was down below her window, throwing pebbles so she'd open up. Who'd have thought?

"I need to talk to you," he said. He didn't even bother whispering. This was a boy who was used to getting what he wanted. He didn't have the courtesy to whisper or act a little polite, so Iris's neighbors wouldn't hear him.

"You need to talk me?" Iris pointed at her chest.

"Yes, you. What's so strange about that? Come on, come down now," he said, as if he was just telling her about the weather.

"No, I am not coming down," Iris said. "You can't just knock on my window and tell me to come down."

"Oh." he mopped his forehead. "I'm sorry. I guess I have crossed the line. Look, there is something important I need to tell you. I think I discovered something."

"Is that who I think it is?" Zoe craned her neck from under Iris's arm. "Hi Colton," she waved at him. "It's Zoe, from class."

"Zoe," he pretended to know her. "But of course. How are you?"

"He asked me how I am doing," Zoe giggled at Iris.

"I heard," Iris pulled her back.

"I'm sorry if it's a bad time," Colton said.

"Wait," Iris said. "We're coming down."

"Thank you," Colton said. "I'm sorry again. It's just, I've never really known a girl as just a friend, if you know what I mean..."

"Colton," Iris warned him. "Stop talking. You're blowing it. I am coming down. Let's see what this is about, Zoe."

"Are you seriously going down without taking a snapshot of him standing down by your window?" Zoe had already pulled out her phone. "You realize this isn't going to happen again, right? This is practically history in the making."

"Shut up Zoe." Iris pulled her out of the room.

Colton stood waiting next to his sports car when they arrived, the exact time Cody came chugging up on his motorcycle.

"Cody!" Zoe waved.

Cody came up wearing a tuxedo that looked a size or two bigger than it should. Iris thought Zoe should later teach him to wear a size that fit, if this ever worked out between them. Not that Zoe was the best of dressers, but certainly better than Cody. Also, she wondered how Zoe was going to ride on the motorcycle with her new dress.

"Bro," Cody nodded at his brother.

Colton nodded back silently, a little confused.

"So this is going to be a double date?" Cody clapped his hands together with enthusiasm. "So cool. Two brothers, and two... you're not related, right?"

"This isn't a double date, Cody." Iris was firm about it, hoping her reddened cheeks wouldn't show in the dark of the street.

"Yeah, really. It isn't," Colton confirmed, looking a bit fazed.

"Alright," Cody tried to think of what this was then. "So what is it? Is Iris coming with us, so she makes sure I am not a serial killer?" he turned to Zoe. "Because I'm not. Really. Ask Colton."

Colton looked as if he wished he could disappear. This was just an awkward situation. "Yes, really. He isn't a serial killer. A serial hacker maybe, but not a killer." Colton said, rather mockingly.

Iris almost laughed out loud at how different the two brothers were. One was calm as hell, and the other was lucky he could still stand straight.

"Colton just came to talk to Iris about something," Zoe explained to Cody. "It's pure coincidence."

"Ah," Cody raised a genius finger. "It must be about the..."

"Cody," Iris snapped. "You should go now. You two are late for Vera's birthday party."

"You're going to Vera's birthday party?" Colton looked too eager to know. So unlike him, Iris thought.

"Yeah," Cody said. "Aren't you coming? You're the party animal."

"I was," Colton said. "But I'll pass. Is she going to be eighteen tonight at twelve?"

"No," Cody pouted. "She's going to be eighteen two years from now, when Uranus clashes into Mars. Of course, she'll be eighteen tonight. You're funny bro." He pretended he was opening an invisible door for Zoe, then ushered her to ride behind him. Iris watched Zoe play princess, pretending there was actually a door.

"Shouldn't you get a cab?" Iris wondered. "Zoe's dress is going to get messed up on that thing."

"It's not a motorcycle," Cody said, starting the engine. "It's a unicorn."

Colton laughed in a good way. "Have fun, bro," he said, and waved goodbye to Cody's chugging unicorn. Although Colton was smiling, Iris had sensed his concern about Vera and her birthday. She wondered about what he'd discovered.

16

"Before you tell me anything, you need to understand that you can't come throwing pebbles at my window again," Iris sat in the comfortable passenger seat of Colton's car. Like most things in The Second, it was a shade of shiny metallic silver. There was no point in asking how much it cost.

"I understand," said Colton. "I just had to tell you something."

"You said that before," Iris wondered why she treated him a bit too bluntly. She must have been pressured by his sudden visit. "What is it?"

Colton pulled out Eva's picture with Vera and Elia. It took a second for Iris to connect the dots. "You came to show me that the three of them knew each other?"

"Two of them were called by the Beasts," Colton said. "I think maybe Vera is next."

Iris pondered the thought in her head. She was dying for something to connect the girls the Beasts took, but the three of them being friends wasn't that much of a connection. "I think it's just coincidence."

"Eva and then Elia, in two consecutive weeks?"

"I bet Eva has many other pictures with other girls that have not been called," Iris pointed out. "Besides, Vera is going to be eighteen in a couple of hours, and Elia was taken yesterday. Never have the Beasts taken two girls in such a short period. No girl is going to be taken again for five days, at least."

"I didn't know that," Colton said.

"Everyone knows that," Iris said. "Maybe you don't know it because you're a boy, or maybe because you never really cared, before Eva." She tried not to meet his eyes saying the last part, but she had to be honest about it.

"You're right. I never cared about anything, but me," Colton said, looking disappointed with himself. The boy had been scoring point after point with her. She wondered if he knew that, or if he even liked her in the slightest.

"So that's all? I think I should go," she said. Sitting with him in the same car already made her dreamy.

"I know you think that I am a bad person, but believe me, I'm trying to be a better man," he said. Iris was going to kiss him violently and tell him he wasn't that bad, but then she discovered it was all in her head. The boy was grieving. "I've discovered something else. Something important about the Pentimento idea."

"Yeah?"

"I'll have to show it to you myself," he started the engine and clicked the doors closed automatically, without even asking her. "Buckle up, Iris."

17

Colton drove toward the Great Wall near the bakery house. He parked his car in a VIP garage that was tangent to where the robots stopped anyone from going further, a mile before the wall. Iris didn't comment as she saw him use his father's ID to enter the garage as a VIP. Inside, he parked the car, and then ushered her to walk the long mile beside him, directly toward the wall.

"I am going to assume you stole your father's ID, and that what we're doing is totally illegal." Iris said.

"Totally," Colton said, walking. "I'm sorry to put you through this, but you have to see."

"Don't be sorry," Iris smiled. "I told you, I like illegal. I am starting to really wonder why I haven't been expelled from school so far."

Colton laughed admiringly at her. Iris's heart sank to her feet. Did this guy admire her somehow? *Of course not, Iris. He is just a rich brat, and you're a poor amusing doll. Do you think he really doesn't know you like him?*

"Don't you care about breaking anyone's rules?" Colton wondered.

"You're breaking them too."

"Going with you to the Ruins was my first law-breaking endeavor, actually."

"I'm starting not to like you now," Iris said. One point down, she thought.

"Does that mean you like me at least a little bit?" Colton didn't look at her. He kept walking straight ahead. She couldn't see his face clearly. Did he really mean it?

"That's beside the point," Iris said.

"Of course," he swallowed. "I have to admit, it felt so good breaking the rules though."

"And stealing your father's ID?"

"Much better," Colton laughed. "I asked my grandmother, a lovely lady who likes to tell jokes about my father when he was a kid, about the Great Wall. She was kind enough to tell me that the Council members had access to the Great Wall and beyond it. She is in a wheelchair, and she winked at me, as if wanting me to go see for myself."

"I'm not surprised how the Council members have access to the Great Wall," Iris said. "But how do they get to the Ruins? Do they just walk through?"

Iris followed Colton through the empty mile leading to the Great Wall, which looked as if it were unreachable. No matter how close they walked to it, all Iris saw was the horizon of land underneath a never-ending sky.

"Yes." Colton stretched an arm toward the sky. It disappeared behind it. "The Sky is a hologram. An illusion. Some brilliant technology where you'd think it's a far away sky, when you can just walk through it and reach the Ruins."

"I knew that, but I never thought you could just walk through it."

"Crazy technology, right?" Colton said, and strode forward, half of his body now buried behind the hologram of the sky. "The birds are an illusion too. The Beasts don't want anyone to know that. That's why there are guards a mile before the Great Wall. Now, let's walk in. We don't need the tunnel under the bakery."

Reluctantly, Iris followed Colton, and walked through the Great Wall. It felt like walking into a huge sponge, or a car wash. She could feel the texture of the hologram wet on her skin, but only for three or four feet. Then the world darkened again, and they were in the Ruins.

"Is that what you wanted to show me?" she asked.

"Of course not."

18

Iris took some time treading through the Ruins, as if for the first time. She stole a brief look behind her at the back of the Great Wall, then continued walking. It was interesting how entering the same place from a different door changed how she saw things. It was like discussing the same subject from a newer point of view.

"Do you have any explanation why the Council created the Wall that way?" Iris asked Colton.

"All I can think of is that they needed to get in and out of the Ruins repeatedly. Why, I have no clue," Colton said. "What I'm really concerned about is their use of such an illusion, and by that I mean the Great Wall. Can you imagine that the sky and horizon we see from afar while driving each day is an illusion?"

"I am still trying to digest it, Colton," Iris said. "But what did we expect them to do? Build a giant steel fortress of a wall and inform everyone that The Second is nothing but a close-minded society, surrounded by the aftermath of the mistakes of our past? The wall completes the lie we live in here under the Beasts' order."

"Which brings me to the thing I had to show you," Colton said.

"Colton. I feel like I've opened a hole in your mind when I showed you the Ruins."

"You did," he said, pointing at a row of two-story buildings he wanted to go to. "I won't back off now. I owe it to Eva."

Although it wasn't reasonable, Iris could have felt jealous now. But she admired Colton instead. Even though she'd doubted his relationship with Eva had been truly from the heart, he wasn't going to let her misery go unnoticed. It was clear that if she was still alive, and he could find a way to save her, Colton was going to do so.

"So what do you want to show me? And what does it have to do with what I just said?"

"In a minute," Colton said. "We're getting closer. I've been trying to get to the bottom of this thing, and discovered that the key to unlocking this mystery is to know what really happened before the Beasts."

"Some kind of war," Iris suggested as they stopped in front of the two-story house. "I imagine it was a terrible war that destroyed the sky above and turned it gray." Iris glanced up for a second, then looked around her at the mess of the Ruins. "The kind of war that killed people. And damaged plants, turning them into horrible black seeds bending awkwardly out of the earth's soil? A war that disfigured every animal species and turned them into some new-born monsters?" Iris was speculating from the top of her head. She'd never really thought much about it. Someone had destroyed the world, and the Beasts had restored it for some unknown reason.

"Here is a big part of the answer to what happened," Colton waved the black light instrument at the house's wall to show her a new Pentimento he'd found.

"You've been seriously working this out," Iris was impressed. "And you've already searched the Ruins for other Pentimentos?"

"Just look," Colton insisted.

The part of the peeled paint from under the new paint showed another old graffiti. It was written on a whim, with an awkward angle upward and to the right, and not all of it was visible. Only the words "rising."

"Rising?" Iris grimaced.

"Come here," Colton ran eagerly to the next building, splaying the light on another wall where it said, in the same handwriting and reddish spray, "upris."

"And here," Colton's enthusiasm was contagious. He continued showing her the red paint on most of the buildings on this street. It was clear that the word written underneath was "uprising."

"I get it, Colton. Stop." Iris calmed him down. His eagerness to know what happened to Eva was exhausting her mind. "So there was an uprising before the Beasts came. It's not that surprising. If nations managed to mess up the world so bad, then there definitely were people who wanted to make things right."

"The question is, an uprising against who?" Colton said.

"The government, I guess," Iris speculated. "Whatever was equivalent to the Council of their time."

"You said it yourself, the Council," Colton said.

"You lost me now. What are you saying?"

"Remember the saying 'humans only see what they...?' I don't think it was written by humans. I think it was written by the Beasts."

"That doesn't make sense, Colton." Iris said. "Why would they?"

"What if the Beasts never really arrived, Iris?" Colton held her by the shoulder. It was a firm grip, but it didn't hurt.

"Are you saying there are no Beasts?" Iris found herself staring up at the gray sky, then back to Colton with his intense blue eyes. "Are you saying the Beasts are an illusion like the Great Wall? That they are simply made up by humans? The Council?"

19

Although everyone else neglected them at the party, Zoe was having a great time with Cody. He was as clumsy and awkward as they come, but he was making a great effort to impress her. She'd imagined he'd tried to make an impression on Iris as well, but it didn't bother Zoe. She figured he was just lonely. Something told her that boys like him stick around if they fall in love. They'd be lonely enough to cherish being with someone they appreciate, and sharing a life together.

Except for a few glasses spilled, a little tripping while entering the birthday, and talking non-stop, Cody was okay.

"You know what we are in this party?" Cody whispered to her, trying his best to hold onto his glass among the crowd. He told her he never drank out of such fancy glasses, and that he preferred paper cups. Even better, drinking straight from bottles.

"What are we?" Zoe snickered, lowering her head. She was a bit taller than him. Talking to Cody felt as if they both shared a secret conspiracy which no one else knew about. Zoe didn't like conspiracies when talking to Iris. But with Cody, it was great fun.

"To Vera and her friends, we are the Beasts." Cody said.

Zoe furrowed her eyebrows.

"Think of it. The Beasts are probably the aliens. And what are aliens? Those strangers whom we fear, but are probably more intelligent than us."

"Ah," Zoe laughed. "So that's why. You think the Beasts are cool?" Zoe wondered.

"I know we hate them, and we should. In fact, I think we haven't even seen the bad, menacing things they want to do to our kind yet. But if it comes down to cool and intelligent, I'd say they must be. Or why do we permit them to rule us?"

"Iris's dad always says that the foolish men usually rule because the smart ones don't really need the attention." Zoe snuck a look at the birthday girl, Vera, who'd invited her, but never really spent any time speaking with her. She'd just said hi when Cody and Zoe arrived, bestowed an infuriating look upon Cody's uncool shoes, then walked away. Zoe thought she'd just wait until the clock struck midnight, then leave. Iris was right, coming here was a mistake. Thankfully, there was Cody.

"I like Iris's dad, but I beg to differ on this one," Cody said. "If there are anyone who are fools it would be us, the citizens, for accepting to be ruled by the *fool*."

"But don't you think the Beasts are ugly creatures, or they would have shown themselves to us?" Zoe said.

"Ugly to us, maybe."

"What is that supposed to mean?"

"In our perspective as a human, the Beasts could be ugly to us. They could be considered beautiful to their kind."

"This means in their perspective, they might consider us ugly." Zoe thought Cody's mind was off the rocker. She liked off the rocker.

"Wow. Don't get me started in this kind of philosophy." Cody said. "You can't handle me."

"Try me," Zoe winked, then suddenly realized she was flirting with Cody. She remembered how Iris always encouraged her to do whatever she wanted.

Actually, Cody shrugged when she said that. He gulped on his drink as if it was some magic potion, then said, "Okay. Here is something that would boggle your mind. Imagine this: the Beasts think of us as ugly creatures. I mean surely. Look at us. We have two eyes. Two legs and two arms. This might strike them as ugly, since they probably have one eye, one toe, and six arms. And they are green."

Zoe laughed. "So?"

"So imagine if our looks aren't what bothers them," Cody's face knotted and a warning finger appeared from nowhere. "Imagine if what bothers them... what makes us ugly to them, isn't our looks."

"What?" Zoe pondered. "Since when isn't ugliness related to looks?"

"Imagine if the Beasts don't like our actions; the way we do things. Our hate and envy, and everyday stupidity."

"That's a unique thought." Zoe began thinking if she should kiss Cody tonight. He had such a dangerous mind. She liked boys with dangerous minds.

"What if the Beasts really see through us?" Cody said. "What if they know how shallow we are," he pointed at Vera, who seemed offended by it. Cody acted fast and pretended he was waving at her. Vera felt unsettled and looked away. "What if the Beasts know how illogical we are? What if they see all those silly rules we follow like sheep everyday. What if they noticed that we mostly do nothing but hurt each other all day long? What if this makes us really ugly to them?"

"I never thought about it that way. I understand why you and Iris clicked right away," Zoe considered. "But you sound like you're defending them."

"Not at all," Cody said. "I know by heart that they are evil, and that taking the Bride is only the start of the bad things they will do to us later. All I'm saying is that, from a cosmic point of view, it's really hard to tell who is beauty, and who is beast."

"From a cosmic point of view?" Zoe laughed again and held her glass up. "Let's make a toast."

"I love toasts." Cody said. "Let's toast to Vera the obnoxious." He lowered his voice. "It's only fifteen minutes until the clock strikes midnight and Cinderella, I mean Vera, turns eighteen and escapes the Beasts' wrath."

"You sound like you doubt it," Zoe said.

"Who knows?" Cody grinned. "The Beasts work in mysterious ways."

20

Iris and Colton sat on one of the building's rooftops in the Ruins, mostly waiting for the clock to strike twelve, so they'd know if Colton's theory was plausible. Bully or not, no one deserved to be taken as a Bride for the Beasts, Iris had told Colton. She thought that the more time they spent together, she began to have a stronger influence on him. Who'd have thought Colton Ray would be dangling his barefoot feet from a building in the Ruins like her? He looked too attractive doing it.

"You know I haven't seen any of the slugs who are supposedly inhabiting the Ruins?" Iris said, looking through her binoculars, scanning the area for any dangers.

"I'm not sure we want to meet one of them," Colton said. "I did have the strange feeling though that someone was watching me while I was here before."

Iris lowered the binoculars. "Me too," she said. "I always have the feeling of someone watching me here in the Ruins, but I have never actually encountered anyone."

"You think the Council's watching us now?" Colton said.

"I think the Council would have caught us already if they were. They never hesitate putting someone in jail, and I don't see the point in risking us telling everyone else about our findings."

"We don't really know much if you think about it," Colton said. "We know almost nothing. We're just rummaging in a pile of secrets, unable to pull one we're certain of."

"You're right," Iris shrugged her shoulders. "You think if the Beasts take Vera, it could lead us to something?"

"If they do, then all we have to do is search thoroughly, and find out what these girls have in common."

"Well, the three of them are beauties." Iris said, rather mumbling.

"What that's supposed to mean? You have this incredibly beautiful vibe about you. If I were a Beast, I'd have taken you already. "

Iris was about to swallow her tongue, shying her eyes away from Colton. It was as if she wanted to disappear into a private room of her own and do a happy dance, somersault a couple of times, and then come back to him. Colton thought she was beautiful. In what world was this possible? Ironically, in a world ruled by Beasts.

"Are you okay?" he said. He looked a little uneasy. Was it possible he was a bit shy? No way. He'd just told her, standing by her window, that he wasn't used to having girls as buddies. Of course, all girls wanted to play Barbie with him, Iris bit her lower lip.

"Never been better," she leaned back on her elbows, pretending that confidence was her middle name.

"It's only two minutes til twelve," Colton said.

"Are you planning to take me to the ball and find my glass shoe then?" Iris flirted.

Colton didn't reply. He raised his head from his watch and smirked slightly. It was the best eye-locking moment so far. Short, but meaningful. The boy wasn't really annoyed by her presence, like how she'd thought things would turn out before.

"Are you ready to dance with me?" Colton said.

Wow. Was he flirting back?

"As we're waiting for the clock, I wanted to tell you something," Colton said.

Iris glanced at her position and thought it was a very kissable one. All Colton had to do was lean over and kiss her.

What kind of girl are you? The voice inside her head annoyed her. *He just lost his girlfriend a short while ago. Besides, he said nothing about liking you. He could tell any girl she is beautiful.*

Iris thought her annoying inner-self was right, but she was excited and maybe a bit dreamy. But she had to be, she was seventeen. She could be taken by the Beasts any day of the year, and her life would be over. In a flash. Would she care then if she'd flirted with Colton or not? Iris was tripping on her thoughts. She'd never thought she'd be taken as a Bride herself, and she wondered why the thought had never occurred to her. Maybe because she hadn't had anything going on with Colton before. He hadn't even known she existed. But now, the mere possibility of having him in her life made it a precious life. Not that she couldn't take care of herself, but with Colton, life seemed meaningful. Where would she find a hot boy who's actually interested in all the weird things she liked?

Iris's head was about to melt from the high voltage of thoughts. She noticed she hadn't answered Colton.

"Iris?" He leaned closer. "Is something wrong?"

Iris kept looking in his eyes, distracting trances clouding her thoughts, her fear of being taken any moment crashing in on her. And with Colton near her, she felt a great desire. Not just for having him. But for life. It seemed so precious and so short all of a sudden. She ended up doing something shockingly beautiful.

21

Colton didn't have enough time to register what Iris was doing. She answered him in the most unexpected way. It was faster than lightning and mind blowing, but in a beautiful way. It was nothing like he'd imagined. As he was leaning over her, making sure she was alright, Iris pulled his neck closer to her with one hand. She did it fast, a bit too aggressive, as if her life depended on it. She pulled his face in until their lips met, and she kissed him.

Colton had never been so vulnerable. Many girls had done this to him before. He knew he was an attractive guy. He even liked his looks in the mirror. But Iris was different. Never had he felt his heart race this way. He wanted this so bad, but it was a little scary she initiated it.

What a crazy girl, he thought. No wonder I make excuses to be next to her. And I've only known her for three days.

Colton and Iris's lips stuck together for a while. She was inhaling him, and he did the same. He thought she'd never let go of him, until they were both out of breath. And he liked it.

But then Eva's image fluttered behind his eyes, right in his mind's eye. Something didn't feel right. Slowly, he pushed Iris away from him.

"I-I'm sorry," she felt embarrassed. "I mean, I don't know why I did this. I-"

"Iris," Colton shushed her. "It's alright. I liked it."

"You did?"

"It's just, I can't right now," Colton said. "I admit, I like you a lot. But I can't open up to anyone, before I am sure I did my best to help Eva--if I even can help her. But I need to make sure I didn't just forget about her and go on with you."

"Did you love her?" Iris leaned forward. Colton knew she wanted to talk about how he came to like her so fast, but she probably was embarrassed enough not to bring it up now. He had no explanation why he liked her anyway, so it was for the best not to talk about it.

"Of course I felt something for her," Colton said. "She was my girlfriend. It's just--you wouldn't understand."

"Try me." Iris patted him gently.

"Boys like me, with my family's history, with all the money we own, and with what I am expected to be in life, we don't really choose the girls we end up with. It surely looks that way, but it isn't always true."

"How so? I thought you could have any girl you wanted. Actually, I know this for a fact. You just need to spend ten seconds in the girls' bathroom."

Colton laughed. "You shouldn't be telling me that. Anyhow, I can get most of the girls I want, as long as they're in my league. I don't get to meet girls from other factions or classes, and choose someone I like to spend my time with, like you," he raised his head to meet hers and touched her cheeks briefly, before pulling away again, remembering Eva.

Colton watched Iris speechless and confused. She must have never thought this about him, but he understood completely. Before he could open his mouth again, his phone beeped. It was twelve o'clock.

Both of them stared at each other, then placed their hands behind their ears, making sure they hadn't missed the sound of the Horn of the Beast.

"No Call," Iris said.

"So Vera is alright," Colton noted. "And we're back to square one. There is no relation whatsoever between the girls."

Iris sighed, and Colton patted her now. She pulled his hands in hers. "Don't worry. We'll keep looking until we know what happened to Eva," she said.

"Damn," Colton fisted his other hand. "I don't think I am doing my best. I am not using my mind the right way. There is something missing here. If only one of the girls ever came back to tell us what happened to her..."

"That's practically daydreaming, Colton," Iris said. "It will never happen."

"Think, Colton, think." He pulled his hand away from her and put both on his head. "Think," he said, one more time. He could sense Iris worrying about him, not knowing what to do. "What if the uprising in the past wasn't against the government or the old Council?" he wondered.

"Then who would it have been against?" Iris said.

"The Beasts," Colton gazed back at Iris. "What if the Beasts always ruled, and the uprising was simply against them, just like the little revolution going on now?"

"That's one heck of a thought." Iris didn't look keen about it. "Are you saying the Beasts ruled the Earth since whenever?"

"Since it began," Colton suggested. "What if they created the Earth? What if it's only a playground, and they are watching us up there?" Colton stood up and talked to the gray skies. "You see us. Don't you? You're laughing at us. This is only some kind of a TV show for you. Right?"

"Calm down, Colton," Iris stood up, clinging to his arm.

"The uprising could have just been people like you and me, people that felt that this world doesn't make any sense." Colton told Iris. "The Beasts could be some kind of ugly, horrendous species that have great powers, but no looks at all. Something like that." He paused for a moment. "Maybe they created this place and made fun of the people here. Others like us may have discovered this and rose up against them in the past, so the Beasts punished them and destroyed Earth."

"If so, then why did they create us?" Iris didn't look convinced in the least.

"Maybe we're only a better version of who lived here before," Colton said. "Like a version 2.0 of your favorite software or phone. We are their product, and they are enhancing us."

"Please calm down, Colton," Iris's eyes were moistening. "You're just feeling guilty about Eva. If the Beasts could create beautiful people like us, why didn't they fix themselves? Are you even listening to yourself?"

Colton took a deep breath. Iris made more sense than whatever his mind came up with. She was right. He was only maddened that he had no clue what happened to Eva. And now that Vera wasn't taken, there weren't enough leads to follow. He felt lost.

"Maybe we should just let it go." Iris said. Colton knew she didn't mean it. She'd just said it to calm him down. "Maybe we should just accept it like everyone else, or we'll go mad. Believe me, I've lost it many times thinking about this."

"But..." Colton said, holding her in his arms. The mere presumption that she was about to cry now, broke his heart. He knew by now that he didn't want this to happen to her. That he wanted to protect her.

"But what?" she leaned into his big chest.

"What if you're next?" Colton squeezed tighter. The thought of losing her too drove him crazy.

"I don't know, Colton," she said. "I don't know. I don't want to even think about it."

For the first time, Colton realized that as strong and stubborn as Iris pretended to be, she was just as afraid as any other seventeen-year-old girl in The Second. Something told him that he'd soon have to fight the Beasts for her.

22

Colton drove Iris home in his metallic car. Frankly, Iris felt like choking in it. Spending too much time in the Ruins, she'd started hating everything shining in silver, everything that felt inhuman to her. The Ruins weren't that bad, she'd been thinking along the way. Yes, they were grayed out and damaged, but there was some kind of unreasonable but beautiful, hope there. Iris imagined herself fixing the Ruins; planting seeds, building new houses, and bettering the soil. All the things she couldn't do here in The Second, because the Beasts decided on behalf on everyone. Hell, the red roses grew in the Ruins, through all that mess. They never made it in The Second, where roses were plastic, almost metallic.

Colton had been silent all the way back. She thought she'd pushed it too far, kissing him. Seriously, what girl did that? What was she thinking? She just couldn't help it. And although it looked like she were bold, pulling him closer to her lips, she was as vulnerable as newborn birds, waiting for their mother to come back and feed them in the nest.

But Colton proved to be a smart boy again. He drove with one hand, while he stretched his other to hold Iris's hand. It was like he was telling her he wanted her, wanted to be with her. But she had to respect the time he had to give to Eva.

Iris understood that. In all truth, she'd crossed the line so many times when it came to Eva. People don't just get over girlfriends so easy, even when they were the likes of Eva and Vera.

"We've arrived," Colton stopped the car in front of her house and faced her. Iris said nothing. This was supposed to be the moment of the goodnight kiss. But it wasn't going to happen. Things were escalating so fast and she worried that maybe they were only hanging out together out of fear, not love. "I'll see you tomorrow?" Colton said. He sounded as if he were unsure he would.

"Tomorrow it is," Iris said, and pulled her hand gently away. "No goodbye kiss, huh?" she couldn't help it. She'd never acted like that before.

Colton laughed with closed lips. It was as if he was afraid if he opened them, she'd pull him closer again. "No," he shook his head playfully. "You have a best friend to call and gossip to about your adventures today. I know how this works in the girl world."

"I don't think so," she said. "It's late, and Zoe hasn't called me. I guess things are going well between her and Cody."

"Oh. So my younger bro scored big time tonight," he fisted his hand in the air and bit his lip.

"You're bad," Iris laughed. "Don't say that about my best friend."

"Is she really your best friend?" Colton said, his eyes scanning Iris's face in a gentle way. No one had ever looked at her that way, with all this care and eagerness. In fact, Colton's look was as good as a kiss for the night.

"I'd die for her," Iris said. "You have no idea how many times she's saved my ass."

"This ass?" he pointed at it.

"Come on," Iris said and got out. "You're really bad."

"Iris," he held the door before she shut it.

"Yes?" she tilted her head down.

"Next time we kiss, let me make the first move," he joked. "Please?"

Iris nodded, her face fluffy and red, like pink cotton candy. She shut the door and walked to her house.

Inside, Charles was sitting on the couch, watching the news. Rarely had Iris seen him watch the news, unless there was something of great importance happening in The Second.

"Hey dad," she said.

He replied by raising the volume. He was watching the news and looked worried.

"Is something wrong?" she wondered, and sat next to him.

"The Council is arresting any family that is still mourning their Bride," he said. "Any family that still has memories, pictures, evidence, or hasn't emptied the daughter's room after being Called by the Beasts."

"That's strange," Iris said. "I always imagined the Beasts knew about the few families not fully complying with the rules. I thought they just didn't bother that much. It's inhuman to think that every family can just pretend they've forgotten their daughter."

"The Beasts are inhuman, Iris." Charles said, still watching the news. "Your assumption is pointless."

"You're right, dad. But, why now?"

"I don't know why now, but I know they are arresting any family keeping a red rose somewhere in the house."

"What?" Iris's heart sank to her feet. "Our red rose?"

Charles nodded. "There are no red roses in this world but those you found in the Ruins. Red roses are evidence of breaking the rules now. It's considered to be the weapon used in a crime."

"Do they know about us?" Iris touched her father's face and pulled it slightly in her direction.

"Yes," Charles said. "They know there is a girl who gives a red rose to the families of the Brides. A girl they are looking for now." He had tears in his eyes. "I shouldn't have agreed to do this. I'm afraid they are going to hurt you now."

"But they don't know who I am," Iris said. "I never showed my face to the parents and I always used gloves."

"Do you think the Beasts can't get you if they wanted to? They already know it's a girl who sent the roses. How do you think they knew?" Charles said.

"Well, I run away after I ring the bell every time. Maybe someone saw me and recognized me as a girl. My hair could have fluttered from under the hood."

"I won't let them hurt you. You understand?" He held her face in his hands. Charles had rough hands. Hands that had been scratching, nailing, and digging into paintings for years. Hands of a carpenter, a painter, and a protective father. "I'll say it was me."

"Don't worry, dad," Iris patted his hand on her face. "I don't think they'll catch me." She looked over his shoulder at the TV. The news people were announcing that the possession of such a red rose had been declared prohibited. Illegal. They claimed it was a sign of an unjust uprising, and that the Council was going to stand up to it with no mercy. "This is ridiculous," Iris said. "Can't people of The Second see how beautiful the roses are? Don't they question where they really came from? What happened to these people?"

Iris finally retired to her bed after what she'd thought of as a day full of surprises. She thought she'd take some time, counting the stars outside her window, thinking of Colton. Wasn't this supposed to be one of the best parts of being in love--at least, on the verge of falling in love, she hoped?

But Iris was wrong. Going to bed didn't mean the day had ended. Her phone beeped, and for some reason she winced in her bed.

It was a message from Zoe. It was short and to the point. And most shocking: "Help me!"

"She's going to be alright," Cody stood before Iris and Colton. He was blocking them from entering Zoe's room in the Downtown Hospital. He had called Colton to tell him about the horrible incident.

"What happened? I don't understand." Iris panted.

"It was Vera and her friends," Cody said, ashamed that he couldn't save Zoe. "They hurt Zoe."

"What about them?" Colton said in his usual calmness.

"Look, I'm sorry," Cody said to Iris. "I should have helped her. But the boys, Vera's friends, locked me in the room."

"You're making this worse, Cody," Iris said. "Tell me what happened to Zoe."

"Vera and her friends pulled a prank on her," Cody said. "A horrible one. I told Zoe that I had a bad feeling about it, but she didn't listen to me."

"Okay," Colton held his younger brother by the shoulder. "Take a deep breath and tell us what happened."

"Zoe and I were going to leave the party after the clock struck twelve," Cody said. "We were planning on going out on our own. We kinda... you know... things kinda clicked between us," Cody said in a faint voice.

"That's good to hear, Cody. What happened next?" Colton took care of the situation.

"Vera suddenly seemed overly nice to Zoe, and asked her to cut the birthday cake for her," Cody said. "As I said, I didn't like it, but Zoe thought she finally was blending in. Even though we'd been talking all night about us not fitting in at the party. If she just had stopped being so naïve and optimistic. Also, she and I were having fun, so she was kinda vulnerable, and let her guard down."

"Okay?" Iris said, her heart still racing, wanting to see Zoe right away.

"Once Zoe walked to the cake and held the knife in her hand to cut it, Vera turned all the lights off. The switches didn't even work anymore. I tried them. It was all planned. I heard Zoe trip, but that wasn't the worst part. All of Vera's friends had bought those night-vision glasses so they could see in the dark and they must have started scaring Zoe and poking her."

Iris and Colton flushed with anger, but they were speechless. It was hard imagining someone would do that to Zoe.

"The boys pulled me in a dark room and locked me in," Cody said. "I had no night-vision with me, so I started screaming. I didn't know where I was exactly. All I could hear was Zoe screaming and calling my name. I couldn't do anything about it. I felt so ashamed." Cody didn't cry, but he was shivering. "Then I heard one of Vera's girls scream, and from there on, everything turned into a circus. Someone unlocked the door for me a little later. When I got out, Zoe had scratches and bruises all over her body, and the police had arrived."

"That's a good thing." Colton said. "Who called the police?"

"Probably Vera." Cody said.

"Why would she do that?" Iris asked.

"Because one of Vera's friends was lying on the floor with a cut on her arm. A deep one. My guess is that Zoe was scared, defending herself in the dark, and wounded the girl with the knife that was supposed to cut the cake. It was self-defense, but when the police arrived, Zoe was standing next to the birthday cake with a knife in her hand, spattered with blood, and there was a wounded girl on the floor. You could imagine how it looked in the eyes of the police."

"Unbelievable," Colton shook his head.

"Unbelievable?" Iris snapped at him. "That's all you have to say? Those are your friends who did this. Your league. Your kind."

"But--" Colton tried to speak.

"I'm going to kill Vera," Iris said. "I swear, I am going to hurt her so bad." Iris pushed the door open and entered the room. Zoe was sleeping, sedated with all kinds of tubes connected to her. It didn't look like a critical medical situation, but Iris couldn't imagine what kind of trauma her friend had had to live through. She ran to Zoe and hugged her, crying by her bed.

Cody and Colton followed, standing by the door. "I haven't told Zoe's parents yet," Cody said.

"I'll tell them. Don't worry," said Colton. "You did the right thing, bro. How did the police let you go so easily? Didn't they consider her a suspect?"

"Vera dropped any charges," Cody said. "The whole thing was just to get away with hurting Zoe. They are not interested in putting her in jail. They already have many wounded friends to take care of. Zoe, although blinded by darkness, gave 'em hell."

"Zoe," Iris knelt beside her, in tears. "Talk to me."

"I think we should leave her alone for now," Colton suggested.

"No. You leave us alone," Iris snapped. "You and your brother!" She didn't think twice about how irrational she was sounding. Colton and Cody would never hurt Zoe. But Iris needed to breathe, and the air in the room wasn't enough to hold her anger. Instead of going to Vera and hurting her, she settled on lashing out on the boy she was falling for. "Please leave, Colton," Iris said, without looking back at him. Iris hoped he understood her pleading. "I can't stand you right now." She couldn't neglect the fact that those who hurt Zoe were his friends, the elite students who never cared for Zoe or Iris, sons and daughters of the Council members.

"I understand," Colton nodded. She turned her head slowly forward. She was thankful he didn't burst back into her face. "I just think Cody should wait for you in the hallway, in case you need anything." He turned to his brother, "Don't let her do something she'd regret, Cody," he told his brother. "Hurting Vera will only hurt Iris's future. We have to find a reasonable way to solve our problems. Not by killing each other, as if we live in a jungle."

"Funny you say that," Cody said. "When we're ruled by the Big Bad Beasts in the Sky."

25

Iris spent the night by Zoe's bed. Her parents had arrived and waited outside. Zoe's protective mother wanted to stay with her, but she had the flu, and the doctors couldn't risk Zoe catching it and complicating her situation.

A while later, the night-shift girl entered the room to check on Zoe.

"Is she going to be alright?" Iris asked.

"Don't worry. Physically, she is a strong girl," the nurse said. "We're only hoping she won't suffer from any post-traumatic stress. What she's been through wasn't easy. "

"Poor Zoe. So when will we know that?"

"I'm not sure, but she's not going anywhere until she's better. Are you her sister?"

"I feel like I am," Iris said, "But I'm not. She doesn't have sisters. Her mother is waiting outside, because she has the flu."

"I see." The nurse nodded. "Do you have any idea who visited her once she arrived? The tall, young and attractive fella?"

"Tall? No, Cody isn't that tall. And I am glad you find him attractive."

"I don't think his name was Cody," the nurse said. She was only about two years older than Iris. "While changing shifts, the other nurses kept talking about a boy who came here named Colton. Yeah, I am sure it was Colton, not Cody."

"Yes. Colton was here. He's Cody's brother, and he arrived before me." Iris was puzzled. "What about him?"

"Hmm..." The nurse hesitated. "He was the first one to enter Zoe's room after the accident. That's what I was told by the other shift nurses. They couldn't stop talking about him."

"He is an attractive boy. He is used to that." Iris's lips twitched.

"I don't think that was the main reason they gossiped about him." The nurse looked as if she preferred to leave, realizing she was interfering in a matter not concerning her.

"What do you mean?"

"Look. This is what I heard. Colton came into Zoe's room, and somehow she hadn't been fully sedated yet. She saw him and screamed. The nurses said it was a hysterical scream, as if he were going to hurt her or something."

"Colton? No way." Iris defended him, but then wondered why she'd suddenly felt mad at him hours ago.

"I am sure there is a mistake," the nurse said. "Sorry for bringing it up. I shouldn't have. It sometimes gets lonely on the night shift, and I can't seem to stop talking when I find company." The nurse excused herself and left.

Iris couldn't shake the thought from her head. Why did Colton arrive before her, and why did Zoe scream when she saw him?

26

A little before dawn, Zoe began to moan in her bed. Iris rubbed her weary eyes and sat up alerted next to her, in case she needed assistance or something.

Zoe's eyelids parted slowly. They were heavy and her eyes showing from underneath were reddened and tired. Her eyes didn't move much. They stood fixed on Iris, as if she didn't recognize her. Iris preferred that Zoe would talk first. She didn't know what to say to her.

Zoe's weakened and scarred hand, injected with an IV, crawled from under the sheets toward Iris, who stretched her hand out to her. Zoe clasped hers into Iris's, still staring at her. Her hands were cold, and Iris could sense the fear passing from Zoe's body.

Her eyes, Iris thought. Oh my, her eyes. What's wrong with them? It's like Zoe had seen a ghost.

"You have to rest," Iris had to speak, still gripping her hand. "You're going to be okay, Zoe. I won't leave. We're all here for you."

"I-" Zoe coughed.

"You don't need to speak now," Iris said. "Just rest."

Zoe's cold hand tightened around Iris's so hard, she wondered where she got the strength from.

"I know who the Beasts are." Zoe said. "At least, I know who one of them is."

Iris didn't even know what to say. She blinked her eyes once, unsure if Zoe was aware of her situation or where she was.

"I saw him with my own eyes." Zoe said, her tongue slurring. "He was here, in the room with me."

"Here? When?" Was this real, or was Zoe just hallucinating?

"After I arrived in the hospital, a sudden headache struck me." Zoe said. "It was terrible. So terrible, I couldn't feel the rest of the pain in my body. I told the doctors, but none of them paid any attention to it."

Iris said nothing again. Zoe must have been hallucinating. First she talked about the Beast, and then the headache.

"After the doctors left, the headache got worse," Zoe said, "And then the Beast came into my room."

"Just like that?"

"He asked if I was okay." Zoe said. "I thought he was someone else at first, but then..."

"Then?"

"It was as if I had an epiphany, as if I suddenly could see him for what he really was. I can't explain it, it just happened. He looked so evil. So scary, Iris."

"I," Iris pondered if she should just calm her down, or try to reason with her.

"Don't you get it, Iris? The Beasts live among us. That's how they see us and control us." Zoe's eyes looked painful. It was as if she'd wanted to widen them and stare at Iris, but her eyelids were too weak to do it. "I'm telling you, the Beast came in the room, pretending to be *him*. He was shocked I saw him for what he really is. I screamed and the nurses came in and pulled him out." Zoe craned her head, just a nudge, toward Iris. "They couldn't see him for what he really is." she whispered. "But I did. I bet he still fools you, Iris."

"Fools me? Who is he?"

"Colton," Zoe said, a shiver trembling through her body. Iris could feel it in hers too, like electricity. She had never seen someone so afraid before in her life. "Colton Ray is the Beast. You've always said it yourself. Remember when you said you thought he was one of them?"

27

The next week went very slowly. Iris spent most of her time at Zoe's house. She'd been released from the hospital after the doctors said she was fine. Zoe had been dramatically getting better after the night she told Iris that Colton was the Beast. Iris considered it a heavy sign that Zoe never mentioned it again, as if it had never happened. She'd seen Colton once after the incident, and she seemed fine with him. She even messed with him and told him Cody was much cuter than he was.

On top of her worries about Zoe, Iris had to deal with her father calling her every two to three hours. The man was worried they'd catch the red rose girl whom the Council decided to call "the Beauty." Iris was thankful for the concern, but wished her dad wouldn't worry so much. She really needed to get home to him soon. The man seemed a bit lonely without her.

Zoe wasn't hurt badly, at least not physically. She had proved to be as tough as Iris, if not tougher. Emotionally though, Zoe was devastated--now that the Colton/Beast thing was not an issue for discussion anymore. Zoe told Iris that what truly frustrated her about the night at Vera's house wasn't just the prank. It was that it could have been one of the best days in her life, since she and Cody had kissed briefly, and that she had been enjoying it. Zoe's attachment to Cody seemed to be too much, too soon. But Iris wouldn't tell her. Anything to help Zoe get over the prank was good.

And as if your attachment to Colton wasn't so abrupt and insane, Iris. Colton had been calling, messaging, and even throwing pebbles at Zoe's window, until her parents chased him away. Iris didn't even acknowledge him. Zoe meant the world to her and if she couldn't go and kick Vera's ass, at least she had to stay by her friend.

Cody had visited her twice. He seemed really concerned, and embarrassed he couldn't protect her. After that, Colton ended up sending Iris a text message, complaining about why Cody was welcomed and he wasn't. This was the only text message Iris answered.

"Remember when you said you needed time to get over Eva? I respected that. Now, I need time to feel comfortable with you. I know it wasn't your fault, but I can't help feeling this way. Please understand."

Colton hadn't replied since.

"You should be going to school," Zoe said, sitting up on her bed. Most of her wounds had healed. It was only her enthusiastic smile that was missing.

"I don't care, Zoe," Iris said. "Since when did I? We'll go together. Doctor said you could be back to school the day after tomorrow. That's not far away."

"So you only go to school because of me?" Zoe smiled.

"Actually, yes. I can't think of another reason. It's not like I am fond of learning."

"And Colton?" Zoe said. "Wouldn't you want to go to see him?"

The question rather shocked Iris. Even though she'd seen her joke with Colton the day she left the hospital, his name never came up again. Iris stared into Zoe's eyes. Did she really not remember what happened? Had she been hallucinating? Iris hadn't asked Colton about the incident. It sounded absurd, and wouldn't have helped their relationship at the moment. After being harsh on him, she wasn't going to accuse him of being a Beast. "He's been amazing, Zoe." Iris hid her concerns. In a rare moment, she lied to her friend. "I mean, really. He is someone so different than the personality he portrays in school. It's just that I feel like I am cheating when I am with him. He is one of them."

"That's ridiculous," Zoe said. "The boy has changed since he met you."

You honestly don't remember claiming he was the Beast, Zoe?

"I know, but do you think he won't be friends with his elite bunch of friends anymore? Do you expect him not to talk to them when we go back to school? I guess I am expecting him to do something that makes me know for sure he resents the likes of Vera."

"I think that's not what this is about," Zoe said. "I think this is about him still being somehow attached to Eva."

"Could be," Iris nodded. "But how long will he be like that? I mean, he wants to know what really happened to her. We might never know what happened to the Brides, or who the Beasts are."

"Which reminds me. Who do you think this 'Beauty' is?" Zoe asked. "Did you see the red roses she gave the parents? They're beautiful. I wonder where she got those."

"Glad you think they're beautiful," Iris said. "I mean, I haven't heard anyone say that." Iris had never told her rose secret to Zoe, nor had Zoe seen the Ruins with her own eyes to connect the dots.

"Everyone thinks the roses are beautiful," Zoe ached a little. "They're just like me a couple of days ago, when I denied being curious and wanting to know the truth."

"And now you want to know the truth?" Iris leaned forward.

Zoe nodded silently. "I guess I'm going to act like you. I'll be another Iris outcast, rebelling against the rules that don't make sense, asking who the Beasts are, without giving a damn about the first commandment."

"And may I ask what changed your mind?" Iris was curious. Like always, she wanted to understand, to find a pattern that explained why and how people changed.

"Promise you won't laugh?" Zoe said, her old smile with the dimples in her cheeks had returned.

"I can't promise that. You know I can't lie."

"I'll tell you anyhow," Zoe lowered her eyes. "It's Cody."

"Oh?" Iris grinned.

"I can't explain it, but after we kissed at the birthday party, and after we had such a good time together, I felt so at ease with him. He isn't my knight in shining armor, not a chance. But I realized I don't want a knight in shining armor. I want someone like me, someone who talking to feels like going back home. Someone who likes me for who I am."

"Those are too many statements for a girl that went on a single date with him." Iris said.

"As if you and Colton took your time with liking each other?" Zoe frowned. "You see, there is some kind of a clicking machine that makes the chemistry work. It either happens, or it doesn't. You don't need long to figure it out."

"I agree," Iris said, thinking about Colton. "So Cody is the reason why you decided not to care about rules and do what you want?"

"Yes. Because being with him made me feel like I deserve to know what this world really is. I feel like I have the right to know, because I realized I am going to share this world with someone else someday. I guess being alone makes one passive and not care about things."

"So it's this little thing called love that moves the world after all." Iris remembered how her father still looked at her mother's empty chair, as if she were still with him. Before her mother died, she'd seen them fight and argue on a daily basis. It looked like they couldn't stand each other sometimes. But it wasn't like that. They were deeply in love, and part of it was making each other's lives hell sometimes. It was just how the heart worked. The human heart, Iris reminded herself, wondering if the Beasts knew anything about it.

"By the way, I forgot to tell you something," Zoe said. "I actually discovered this talking to a couple of girls in Vera's party, right before they asked me to cut the cake. Cody was in the bathroom."

"I told you not to go, Zoe," Iris said.

"That's not the point. I learned my lesson," Zoe said. "It's something important. Remember when I told you Elia Wilson was about to become a master tennis player?"

Iris nodded.

"While talking to the girls at Vera's birthday party, I discovered that Eva was about to become one of the best photographers in The Second."

"That's not something so special," Iris said. "A lot of girls are good photographers."

"That's true, but the girls told me that she was truly amazing. And that the Council was waiting to see how good she was going to do in college, to make a star of her. Eva took photographs of the Council members repeatedly. Something that no seventeen-year-old did before."

"So?"

"So the Brides, Elia and Eva, aren't shallow and rich beauties," Zoe said. "I know how we feel about Eva. She definitely deserved to be punished for treating us the way she did. But to be honest, they were special girls."

"I can't believe you're calling them special, with all the bullying they did."

"Here is where you need to be honest with yourself, Iris," Zoe said. "Eva wasn't a good person, but Elia never hurt us. Vera is batshit. What I mean is, we can't generalize ideas. Not all beautiful girls are airheads or snobs. What I'm saying is that the Beasts seem to choose intelligent women, morals aside."

"Saying that these girls are intelligent really bothers me, Zoe."

"I'm not saying this to make you feel bad about yourself. I know you don't like them, and I know none of them bothered attending your mother's funeral. But it's not like you just don't like them. You don't like their kind; the rich, spoiled, sons and daughters of Council members. That why you snapped at Colton. Deep inside, you don't like where he comes from, and you need to fix that, Iris."

"Are you saying I am the bad person now?"

"Of course not. I love you, and I know how special you are. We all have our quirks, our little unjust feelings toward a certain kind of people because of something that happened to us in the past. We are human. We like to generalize things, instead of treating each individual on their own." Zoe inhaled deeply. It was a long speech. "It's okay."

"So, why are you telling me this?"

"Because Vera was friends with both girls. The Beasts took the two girls and didn't take Vera," Zoe said. "Eva and Elia were artists. Vera is shallow, has no hobbies, and loves to hurt others."

"Are you saying there is actually a basis the Beasts choose girls upon?" Iris wished Zoe had experienced her change of heart long ago.

"I can't put my hands on it." Zoe said. "But I have been trying to remember the girls taken last year. I knew a couple of them. They were also special. Gemma Underwood... remember her? She was taken about two months ago. She was one of the best upcoming painters in The Second, and guess what? She came from the same class as ours."

"I remember Gemma," Iris said. "She was really talented, and she wasn't that beautiful actually," she rested her head on her hands.

"Also Tina Remington. She was taken three months ago," Zoe said. "Tina was..."

"One of The Second's best swimmers," Iris interrupted her. "I remember her. But she was a real beauty and she had a great body."

"The point is... most of the girls weren't airheads," Zoe said. "The Beasts aren't choosing their Brides for beauty."

"That's some remark," Iris said. "So what does it mean? The Beasts pick girls with good genes? Not necessarily beauty genes, but talented girls who might produce smart and talented kiddos?"

"We don't know that the Beasts have children with them," Zoe said. "See? That's what I'm talking about. In order to figure out their secrets, you need to have an open heart and be fair in your assumption. You can't assume the girls are for breeding purposes. Maybe they are for something else."

"Maybe the Beasts are cannibals." Iris said.

"I am not going to keep assuming," Zoe said. "Let's start with what we know. They choose special girls and they have designed a wall of illusion to separate us from the Ruins, like you told me."

"That's not much."

"Actually, I think it is." Zoe said. "It's been more than a week and the next call might be tomorrow, or later. If the next girl is as special, this is an important fact."

"Sounds great, friend," Iris patted her. First Colton had the friends theory, and now Zoe had the gifted theory. Somehow, Iris knew both weren't right. "Welcome back. I almost thought I lost you."

"I was going to die, but I had to come back for you, to save your ass like always," Zoe pinched her, and let out a little moan. Her ribs still ached.

"I promise you, I'll kick Vera's ass someday," Iris said. "I think I'll glue Mrs. Wormwood's wig to her head. That would be gold."

"Ouch," Zoe said. "As much as we think we are the good girls, sometimes I feel like we are the bad ones."

Iris laughed. "I have to go now. Dad's been really worried," she said, and walked to the door. But Iris couldn't leave before asking her. "Zoe, do you remember Colton being the first one to visit you when you were first brought to the hospital?"

Zoe squinted, as if trying to see through the memory. "Colton?" she said. "Oh. Yes. I do remember. That was so sweet of him."

"Really?" Iris said. "Do you remember what happened? If he said something to you?"

"That's a hard one, Iris," Zoe laughed. "I was toast. I didn't even remember it until now, when you told me. Don't you think that's strange?"

"Like you said, you were toast," Iris said. "So you don't remember him saying or doing something, reminding you of the Beasts?" Iris shrugged. It was an absurd question.

"You're joking, right? No. I think he told me to be strong and hang tight or something. I do actually remember that he was assuring me that you were on your way. Why?"

"Nothing," Iris said. "I just wondered how fast he arrived before I did. It made me rather jealous. I wanted to be the first person next to you."

28

The conversation with Zoe had melted Iris's heart toward Colton. She'd been hard on him and he didn't give up on her. Still, Iris in her stubborn mode, couldn't pick up the phone and call him. She wondered if she'd inherited this from her mother, who even though she loved Charles, liked everything done in the light of her own beliefs and principles. Also, there was this little uneasiness after Zoe's incident, thinking Colton was the Beast. Iris still had no explanation for what happened. Probably Zoe was in shock and when Colton came into the room, he reminded her of Vera because, in many ways, he was one of them. The only thing that seemed odd was Colton not mentioning the incident. But then again, everyone was in shock and it wasn't important to tell her he saw Zoe first.

Iris climbed down the stairs and picked up her coat and gloves to leave. With her hand gripping the door, she wondered if she'd been blinded by her love towards Colton.

But Colton never ceased to amaze. When she opened the door, he was waiting for her outside, next to his car.

"Before you get mad at me, just hear me out," he said.

"I'm not mad at you anymore," she strode toward him and threw herself into his arms.

"Wow," he hugged her. "I assume Zoe has a hand in this?"

"She does," Iris said, rubbing her cheeks onto his chest. "She persuaded me that I was too hard on you."

"I'm starting to fall in love with her," he joked. Iris hit him lightly on the stomach.

"I have a surprise for you," he said.

"Okay?"

"It demands you trust me, without asking questions." he said.

"I guess I can trust you," she chewed on the words. Why'd he ask her something like that, when she still couldn't get Zoe's incident out of her head? Iris tilted her head and stared into his eyes. Who wouldn't trust those sparkling blue eyes, she thought.

"Are you a girl of your word?" he touched her cheek slightly.

"What do you have in mind?"

"This." He pulled out a scarf made of delicate and fine wool.

"Is that a present?"

"Nope. We're going to blindfold you."

"Hmm..." Iris bit her lip. This was getting both exciting, and worrying. "That's interesting."

"It's just until I drive you to a special place I need to show you." he said.

"I haven't trusted anyone *that* much," she pondered.

"That's the point," he said. "I've been thinking about you all week, and I decided that Eva can't stand between us. I will find out what happened to her and help her if she's still alive, though. But I can't hold myself back from you anymore. I need to be closer to you, Iris. I need to be with you. In your words, I want to peel off all your worries and become your Pentimento. To do so, I want to be sure you trust me."

"Become my Pentimento, huh?" she said. "I get the idea, but I'm not sure if it's the most romantic metaphor you could have come up with."

"Why not? Pentimentos are the original truth of what things were meant to be. I want to know who you were meant to be and will be. I don't want to know Iris the way she wants the world to know her. I want to be closer to you. So close."

"Aren't you worried I might have demons buried beneath my soul?" she said.

"No. I want you the way you are," he smiled. "Shall we?" he showed the scarf again.

Iris nodded, a bit reluctant. Colton began binding her eyes.

"Wait," she stopped him. "But you have to promise me that we're going to an amazing place."

"I promise."

29

Iris enjoyed being guided by Colton. As usual, his hands holding her were warm and gentle. Being blindfolded turned out to be a sensual thing she'd never imagined before. It gave her space to feel things, instead of letting her eyes affect her judgment. It was silly, but she could feel Colton's love through his touch. His grip was firm, yet tender and caring. She enjoyed listening to his breath, a human characteristic overlooked by the Seeing Eye. Sound, when stripped of all affecting colors, held some kind of evidence in it. In Colton's situation, he sounded anticipating, wanting to know if she'd like what he had in store. It occurred to her that Colton was actually giving her the chance to experience something she loved tremendously. Having her eyes blindfolded and then pulling the binding to finally see his surprise was a subtle kind of Pentimento in itself. She wondered if Colton had thought of it that way, or if it was just coincidence.

At some point, after the car stopped and Colton ushered her out, she found herself climbing stairs. It was uncomfortable. Colton made sure she didn't trip somehow by holding her hands.

"Haven't we arrived yet?" She didn't know why she whispered. Maybe because she couldn't hear anyone else's voice nearby.

They were alone.

Colton shushed her, placing a finger on her lips. "You're not allowed to ask questions until we arrive."

Iris complied, although the anticipation was killing her. She wondered if what Colton was eventually opening her eyes to would surpass the enjoyment she was experiencing. In her teen experience in The Second, most things shined from a distance, but weren't as glowing when seen closer.

And again, she thought of Colton's surprise as a type of Pentimento.

What an idea, she thought. Walking blindfolded in the darkness was like staring at the Fragorand painting, thinking the boy and the girl were looking at the Fountain of Love, not knowing the boy was actually a Beast.

Iris's heart skipped a beat as Colton ushered her into a room.

Could Colton really be a Beast? Iris hated herself for thinking this way. But she was now. Her mind brought her most of her troubles in life. If she could just shut it down, she thought, she'd live a much smoother life. The happiest people she knew were capable of shutting their minds off whenever it beeped, like a message from an unknown number.

This is serious, Iris. There are too many coincidences to be overlooked. The Fragonard painting shows a beast underneath. Zoe was hallucinating that she saw Colton as a Beast, and now you found yourself thinking about Pentimento. What if what he's going to show you now is his secret? Will you still love him?

Iris heard Colton hit a button, then the room vibrated. They were in an elevator.

She touched the scarf on her eyes, pretending she was adjusting it. In truth, she couldn't take it anymore. She wanted to take it off. Damn those thoughts in her head.

"No cheating," Colton said in a playful voice.

But why didn't she feel it was playful like before? All that she'd been thinking about seeing without seeing changed all of a sudden, all because of a trivial thought that hit her brain like a virus. How could her perception change so suddenly? The mind and perception, were horrible things. A simple thought could change the looks and feel of someone you had known for some time.

You don't know him. It's only been two weeks or so. Iris began breathing faster.

"Are you afraid of heights?" Colton asked. He sounded worried.

What is wrong with you, Iris? This isn't the sound of a Beast. But then she didn't know how a Beast really sounded. She suddenly realized the Beasts' biggest tricks, the thing that made them the most feared: no one knew anything about them; who they were, or what they looked like. That's why their first commandment was, "Thou shall not question the beast."

"I'm okay," Iris said, dazed and confused. "Are we there yet?"

"We are," Colton said, as she heard the elevator doors open.

Colton helped her out of the elevator and she felt a cold breeze of air circle around her, before almost freezing her fingertips.

"Don't worry about the cold," Colton said. "I will keep you warm."

She let out a courtesy laugh. She trusted him with all her heart, but her mind wasn't on the same page at the moment. And it made her feel like she had a split-personality.

Colton stopped her and rubbed her shoulder. "Once you see it, you will forget about the cold," he said. "Are you ready?"

Pentimento. This was it. The moment when everything is revealed. When the truth comes out. When all our fears and assumptions prove right or wrong.

"I am ready." She nodded. *I'm Iris. My father gave me this name because he expected me to see through the veils of deception, and now I am about to see.*

Slowly, Colton pulled the scarf away. Iris began seeing through the blurring veil covering her eyes. The world still seemed dark. It was nighttime. But the first things that shone through the dark-veiled night were tiny spots in front of her. They were sparkling, like diamonds. They were very close.

They were Stars. Millions of stars. They were so close, she thought she could grab a handful.

She let out a small shriek, staring at her feet. She was worried she was floating in space or something. But there was concrete under her feet. Silver and metallic steel binding it.

She raised her head again, a bit below the stars' level this time. Now she could see it all. She was atop a very high building, overlooking the metallic world they lived in. She was staring at The Second from a point so high, it felt like it was the Beasts' eye.

30

"It's the highest building in the world," Colton said, embracing her from behind. "We're not allowed to be here."

"It's the Council's headquarters?" Iris asked.

Colton nodded, rubbing his chin against her shoulder. "Yes. They call it the Sinai building, the place they rule us from. I stole the magnetic key from my father. I discovered he has three, so he'd probably not figure it out soon enough."

Iris had seen the building many times before, but she wasn't fond of craning her head up high while walking down the streets in The Second. It was so high, it disappeared into the clouds sometimes. "Cody once heard a rumor that the top of the Sinai building was the place where the Council made contact with the Beasts too." Iris said.

"Really?" Colton looked up at the stars. "So they're somewhere beyond the stars then? Are they watching us?" he mocked and waved at them. "I told you they must be watching us."

"Stop it," Iris said, snickering. "It's a ridiculous idea. I just thought I'd tell you what Cody told me."

"It's not ridiculous actually," Colton turned her to face him. He did it, oh, so smoothly, as if they were dancing. "If they are watching us from up there, then they should see why I brought you up here." Colton had that sweet look in his eyes again.

Iris could feel the intensity of the staring in his eyes again. It reminded her of the first time he'd seen her on top of the principal's office. He was staring at her as if she was some kind of wonder. A precious surprise. An everlasting song he couldn't stop listening to. She really wished no other girl in the world had been stared up at this way. Yes, it felt so special, and Iris didn't mind being selfish when it came to Colton's eyes.

"Why did you bring me up here?" Iris said, her voice splintered like glass in the windy snow.

"Remember when I told you the next time I kiss you I wanted it to be my move?" Colton said, as his head was already invading her space. A beautiful invasion.

Iris closed her eyes and waited for the warmth of his lips to save her from the cold. There was no point in talking anymore. Talking sucked sometimes. The arrival of his lips felt like forever, although it had been only a fraction of a second. And with it, an eternal shiver dwelled in her body. It was like a signature, the kind of slight shiver that was never going to leave her body after the kiss, reminding her of this moment when she was so high, she could almost reach the stars.

Colton locked his lips onto hers longer than she'd expected. It was as if *his* life had depended on it this time, and she was losing hers already. Funny how a kiss was the only moment when she didn't mind dying from being out of breath, as long as their lips touched.

Finally, Colton pulled away. Slowly though. Iris opened her eyes, and saw him inhale the cold air around him in his lungs, as if he was drowning.

"I wanted our first *real* kiss to be special," he said. "Just like that."

"Can I tell you something?" Iris said, almost embarrassed she was going to say this.

Colton nodded.

"Stop talking, because I already miss those lips," she pulled him closer again. Colton smirked and as he bent down to her lips again, he showed the middle finger to the

Beasts watching them up there. That's if there were such Beasts in the first place. "Perverts!" he told them, just before Iris could feel that sweet shiver again. She thought it was the best first kiss in history. And if it wasn't, it must have been the highest.

31

Somehow the rain fell heavily after the second kiss, and Colton wondered if the Beasts didn't approve of this relationship. Secretly, he suddenly felt worried about Iris. What if the Beasts decided to make her the next Bride? He shook the paranoid feeling from his mind, as he climbed down with Iris and got into his car.

"I'm driving you home," he said on the way. "But those lips still have unfinished business with me," he smirked.

Iris blushed and preferred to stare ahead at the rainy night. "You didn't have to provoke the Beasts," she joked. "Look at all this rain. We could have spent a little more time up there," she tightened Colton's jacket around her. He had given it to her once the rain started.

"I wonder what provoked them more: the kiss or the finger?" Colton said, holding her hand while driving with the other.

"You still sound like you really believe they were up there watching us." Iris remarked.

"I do," Colton's facial expression sank into a serious mood. "Why do you think they let us do all this research and sneak into the Ruins? They see everything."

"You mean they know about us going to the Ruins? They know about my Pentimento hobby? That can't be."

"Why can't it be?" Colton said. "They see us. As long as there is no major uprising against them, they don't mind letting us dig a little. I think they rather love it. We're like lab rats, just narrow-minded and self-centered humans, and they laugh at us."

"You sound weird tonight, Colton." Iris said.

Colton couldn't find words to respond. She was right. He was feeling a bit weird tonight. But not from the beginning. He had planned this to be a special night. Only something happened to him after they kissed. A horrible idea dawned on him. It was a sudden gut feeling. He was afraid to lose Iris.

Why was he so afraid to lose her to the Beasts all of a sudden?

Because you like her a lot, Colton. This is different from any other girl you've liked. Kissing her felt like selling your soul to her. The little stubborn girl sitting next to you owns you now. Funny that she doesn't know it yet.

Colton knew that he had to solve the Beasts' mystery, or find a way to protect Iris from them until she turned eighteen. If Zoe's speculations were right about the Beasts picking up smart girls with artistic hobbies like Iris had told him, then Iris was definitely on the list. She was smart as hell, and he didn't want to even think about her Pentimento hobby.

"Think about it, Iris," he told her, nearing her house. "Why did they suddenly look for the girl they call the Beauty, the one who gave red roses to the Bride's parents? Why not before? You think with all this technology all around us, it's so hard to know if some parents refuse to wipe their daughter's memory from the face of the Earth? Hell, the Council could tell the way we think from tracking and quantifying what we buy and the kind of TV shows we watch. Our lives are out there on the social networks, our photographs, likes, and daily banter. All this data they gather from our cellphones and surfing the internet. We are watched twenty-four-seven."

"I'm not following."

"The Beasts only declared the red rose as prohibited when the phenomena of the Beauty started to spread, the same time it began to gather a crowd that could start a revolution. An uprising. The same word I found on most of the buildings in the Ruins. There was a huge uprising many years ago, and once the red roses spread to so many houses, they feared the uprising would return."

"So you're still convinced that the Beasts have always been here?"

"I am not really sure of anything," Colton gripped the wheel tighter. "It feels like I am trying to entrap mercury in the palm of my hand. It keeps slipping away." Colton stopped the car in front of her house. He was panting. Iris looked worried. She didn't know why he'd been soaked in fear all of a sudden. He couldn't tell her that the thought of her being a Bride began to drive him crazy. This creepy thought that overtook him, after they'd kissed on top of the world.

He watched Iris lean forward and kiss him briefly. "Goodnight," she said. "This is the best night of my life. I hope it's yours too. Don't think too much, and spoil the memory. Tomorrow we'll continue the search."

Colton nodded, saying nothing.

"I will keep your jacket," Iris said. "I like that it smells of you," she said, and got out.

Colton watched her wave goodbye to him from behind the blurry window with rain trickling down. He drove ahead toward the Ruins, and he wasn't going to tell Iris about it. He didn't want her to worry. He wanted to peel off some more of the phrase "humans always see what they…" Something told him a lot would be revealed if he read the rest of that phrase.

Half an hour later, he was in the Ruins, applying the revealing techniques Iris had taught him. Still, he couldn't read the rest of the phrase. He'd only succeeded in uncovering the first letter from the word following the word "they." The letter was a "V," and it frustrated him that it didn't make solving the rest of the phrase any easier.

Humans always see what they v…?

It didn't make any sense. He was determined to spend the night here, uncovering other letters. He didn't mind if they weren't in order. Just anything that would be a clue, so he could try to figure it out.

As he kept working, he could sense being watched again. Whenever he turned around, he saw no one.

"Whoever you are, I'm ready for you," he yelled at the silent Ruins.

No reply. Just that creepy sense of being watched lurking in the air all the time.

Colton dropped his tool for a second and stared up at the gray sky. There were no stars or clouds here. Just this darkened veil covering the sky above.

"What really happened here?" he sighed. "What kind of war or conflict did this kind of thing to a world people used to live in?"

Asking questions to the still air in the Ruins wasn't going to solve anything. He returned to working on the phrase. The thought of Iris being taken was consuming him with every passing moment. He wanted to tell her that Elia Wilson had also been his girlfriend for a brief time, but couldn't. He was afraid Iris would freak out and leave him. He'd been reckless in the past, but he'd changed now, because of her. But that thought wrapped around him, like a dead man's carcass. If Elia had been his girlfriend, and so had Eva, and both were taken by the Beasts, was he cursed? Were all his girlfriends destined to be taken by the Beasts?

Two days later, the rain had turned into snow, and it fell majestically to the ground. It was a cold, but beautiful day. Zoe's first day back to school, and of course, Iris was with her.

Iris had woken up with an unprecedented amount of energy and love for life. She'd even pondered the thought of trying not to cause any trouble at school, and actually learn something. Why not? She was going to see Colton today.

They hadn't met yesterday because he'd been busy with something, and she'd preferred to spend the cold and rainy day with Zoe, who ended up talking with Cody on the phone the entire time. Iris had decided to sleep in Zoe's bed as punishment for leaving her alone, and also to get her out of the patient mentality.

Zoe's mother had made soup for Iris and interrogated her about who this Cody was. Iris had assured her that Cody was far from being a serial killer, and that she should bless this relationship.

But today, Zoe called Iris to wake her up. "It's time for school," she said on the phone. "I'm so excited."

"You're excited to see Cody, you sneaky liar," Iris rubbed her eyes and jumped out of bed. She put Zoe on speaker as she brushed her teeth and worried aloud that Colton would discover she had a slight gap between her front teeth--as if he hadn't already. Was it also possible that he noticed her hair was slightly thinner on the right side of her head, and that it was stiff when she was a kid?

"Shut up," Zoe said in the speaker. "Colton already likes you. I can't believe we're dating brothers. That's so absurd." she laughed.

"You should listen to Cody going on about Colton. He's more like his Godfather," Zoe added.

"Really?" Iris was beginning to get bored from Colton amazing her with his personality.

"You think the four of us should get married the same day?" Zoe blurted.

"Wow. Where did that come from?" Iris said. "Your head just jumped five years into the future."

"Actually not," Zoe said. "Cody and I are planning to get married in a couple of months."

"You're joking, right?" Iris stopped brushing her teeth.

"No. I'm serious."

"Is that even legal? Say you're kidding, Zoe. You only got to know the boy a couple of weeks ago."

"I'm not kidding. Cody and I have been talking about it a lot."

"Wow. A lot. You make it sound as if you've been planning this huge decision for a year or so."

"Think about it, Iris," Zoe said. "We're all vulnerable here. I could be taken by the Beasts at any moment while I am seventeen. I don't want to regret I didn't do this."

Iris shrugged, staring at her reflection in the mirror. She looked rather awful with the toothpaste crawling out of her mouth, like in a cheap horror movie. But it was that sudden feeling that filled her lungs. Why did she suddenly feel like her time had come to be taken? Was this why Colton had been acting worried yesterday, and the day before?

"Iris?" Zoe said. "Did you drown in the sink?"

"I'm here, Zoe," she said. The toothbrush stuck to her mouth, like a cigarette on wet lips.

"I'm sorry if you don't approve, but Cody will ask my mother to marry me next week. Come on. You should be happy for me."

"I am, of course. You know I will support whatever mad thing you decide to do." Iris said.

"That's my girl," Zoe said. "See you in a while crocodile." She hung up.

Zoe never said stuff like that – that was pure Cody influence.

Iris did nothing but stare at herself in the mirror. Something wicked was about to happen, and she didn't know what. It was a horrible feeling, so present and so illogical.

All the way to school, sitting next to Zoe in her mom's minivan, Iris couldn't shake the feeling from her chest. Something felt like it was coming her way. It was an irrational fear, but it was imminent and grounded. There was no escaping.

"Don't you think it's been too long without the Beasts taking anyone?" Iris asked Zoe.

"It's been nine days," Zoe said. "But it's happened before. One time we waited two weeks."

In class, Zoe followed every word Mrs. Wormwood said. Iris, on the other hand, didn't. She'd been whisked to another world in her mind, looking outside the window at the snow falling. Every second intensifying the crazy feeling in her mind. She'd heard about people capable of sensing danger before it happened. She just never believed it was possible.

Once the bell rang, she hurried to Colton's class. She asked him to talk in private. It didn't help when he looked like he was keeping a secret from her. But Colton loved her. It was only a minute before he told her about his suspicions, that Elia and Eva had been his girlfriends.

"But you must have had a lot of girlfriends before," she told him, standing by a quiet cornerstone next to the playground.

"I did," Colton said. "But..."

"But?"

"What if this is was something that started only with Elia? Elia was my girlfriend before Eva, and Eva before you. Besides, I checked, and none of my other girlfriend were taken. This thing just started with Eva."

"But Elia wasn't your girlfriend when she was taken."

"I thought about that too," Colton said. "Maybe it's going backwards. They took my last girlfriend then the one before."

"The world isn't revolving around you, Colton."

"I know, and I wish I was wrong. It's just that this feeling has taken over me since we kissed. Maybe it's just angst. But seriously, you said you feel it too.

There was no discussing if they were really boyfriend and girlfriend. None of them had uttered the words.

"So what are we going to do?" Iris said, pretending she wasn't afraid. But what was to be afraid of? The Beasts were practically the unknown fate. Nothing was scarier than the unknown.

"I don't know, Iris," Colton hugged her to his chest. A couple of elite students saw this and Iris thought it was ironic. The moment Colton declared she was his in the middle of school should have been one of the best days in her life. Yet, it was one of the scariest moments. "I just have this fear inside me since we kissed on top of the Sinai building."

"You should have told me, Colton. I have the same fear now."

"I didn't want to scare you," he said. "Listen. Whatever happens, I will be there with you," he lifted her head up to him. "I will not give you to them. I will fight for you."

"Fight who?" a single tear escaped her eyes, trickling its way down Iris's cheek. "The Beasts?"

"How can you fight someone you haven't seen, when you have no idea what it really is?" she buried her head in his arms again. "I don't want to die, Colton. I am still so young."

As more tears blurred her vision, her eyes were filled with the Fragonard painting, where the boy was originally the Beast. It wasn't far from the truth now. Colton and Iris were looking at the Fountain of Love, only Colton was the Beast, not because he was evil, but because he was cursed somehow. Maybe Zoe's hallucination was a prediction somehow. Maybe she was warning her unconsciously that being with Colton was going to turn her into a Bride. But how could Zoe have known? It didn't make sense.

Why was this happening to her? Was this what love was, some beautiful form of dying?

"Love is nothing but a Pentimento," she mumbled, not sure if he could hear her. "It looks like something from the outside, while it's something totally different from the inside. And one can only understand this after some time, when the lie on the outside peels off."

"What do you mean, Iris?" Colton said. "Don't say that. You are the world to me. I am not giving up on you. I lo..."

Whatever Colton was going to say was eaten away by the horrible loud blast of the Beasts' horn.

33

While every other girl in The Second sprang to her feet, Iris clung tighter to Colton and closed her eyes. Colton wrapped his arms around her as the snow whiffed its particles onto their faces.

Everyone's phones began beeping and a number of girls starting hooraying nearby. It was a painful sound of celebration to Iris and Colton's ears. Each time girls celebrated, Iris felt closer to fainting. No girl had ever been interested in uttering the number of the chosen one. Maybe out of politeness or fear, who knew?

The beeping spread all around them. Iris couldn't bring herself to check her phone. She hadn't been fond of doing so in the past, why would she now? For a moment, she wished her father hadn't bought her a new phone after the old one broke on Eva's day.

Colton saw a group of girls noticing him and Iris were hugging, instead of checking the phone. The girls had read their messages. They were not chosen and the look on their faces was indecipherable. Was Iris the Bride?

"We have to face this," Colton whispered in her ear. "Let's read the message and see if it's your number. Whatever happens, I am with you."

Iris untangled her arms and clicked on her phone. She raised her head one last time to meet Colton's eyes. They didn't conjure the magical safety they always did when she looked into them this time.

Lowering her head, she scrolled and clicked on the message. The sender was the Council and the number of the Bride was right in front of her face.

Tensed, she thought she'd forgotten her own number for a moment. Then it came back to her. She dared to look at the number on the screen. Well, the first number was like hers. So was the second.

And the third.

Colton began to tense to her reaction.

Thick tears began forming in her eyes. Maybe the fourth wasn't hers.

She was wrong. It was.

And the fifth.

"I can't--" Iris tried her best to inhale. The world seemed void of air all of a sudden. "It's me."

Colton grabbed the phone and read it. This couldn't be true. He wasn't some kind of clairvoyant. Why would the Beasts go after his girlfriends?

He read the number from the beginning, losing breath to each number that matched Iris's ID. But then something happened. The sixth number, and last, wasn't hers.

"Thank goodness," he sighed and hugged her, almost choking her. "It's not you. It's not you!"

Iris freed herself from his embrace and dried her tears instantly, re-reading the number again. She had to make sure.

"It's not me," she said, unable to believe it herself. The happiness numbed her and she couldn't even smile. "I can't believe it."

"We were only paranoid," Colton said, grabbing her shoulders and pulling her closer. Iris stood on her tiptoes and pulled his lips to hers. She needed it now more than ever. Colton kissed her while lifting her up in the air and spinning her around. "I'm sorry I scared you with my stupid interpretations," he said.

Iris sounded like she had hiccups, as Colton lifted her up and down again. "I-I don't understand."

"What don't you understand?" Colton's blue eyes twinkled. "We were wrong. You're not the Bride, and I am not cursed." He waved his eyes toward the sky.

Girls started giggling around them. No one had seen Colton that giggly before.

"And we thought..." Iris hiccupped again. "I was so scared. The first five numbers were just like mine, then..." Iris's hiccups stopped abruptly and her face went pale. Her eyes screamed for help, as she slammed her chest with her hand.

"What's wrong?" Colton wondered. She was acting weird again all of a sudden.

Iris said nothing. Her mouth was agape, staring at Colton with appalled eyes, her tears surfacing again.

"It's not me, but it's..." she stared back at the class she'd left a while ago. "That's why the numbers were so close!" Iris screamed and ran toward the class, slipping away from Colton's hands. "Oh, my. We weren't totally wrong." She said, on the verge of crying. She ran toward the class, pushing students out of her way. This couldn't be. The closer she got, she heard another girl scream. It was a painful scream. It was the scream of today's Bride: Zoe Peterson.

34

If Iris had thought that watching a Bride tread to her death was the most horrifying thing in the world, then she was wrong. The most horrifying thing was watching her best friend walk to the Beasts' ship.

Iris stood to the right with the girls, paralyzed with fear. It was a mystery to her how her feet still held her. She felt like a rose torn into pieces. She was nothing but scattered petals in the air. She couldn't feel the ground underneath her, yet she was still standing.

As Zoe stood there, wearing her wedding dress, she looked at the light coming from the ship at the end of the red carpet. Instead of marrying Cody and wearing the dress for him, she wore it for the Beasts. Zoe was right about wanting to get married so soon, Iris thought. Sadly, it wasn't going to ever happen now.

The look Zoe gave Iris was the look of a dead girl staring at another dead girl. Zoe was dying on the inside, because she was sent to the Beasts. Iris, because she couldn't imagine the world without her best friend. And because she couldn't do crap to save her.

It wasn't like Iris didn't try. She had pulled Zoe with her and ran out of class, jumped into Colton's car as he drove away, trying to escape the police, the Council, and the Beasts.

But in a land where its borders were the Ruins, there was no escaping an illusion. Like Colton had said, the Beasts were up there, watching them, mocking them, and taking their girls. Without the slightest reason at all. The world must have been the table they used to play roulette and humans were the scattered little steel balls.

Colton hadn't even made it to the Ruins. They were caught by the police soon before that, crashing Colton's car and wounding him and Iris. It wasn't a surprise when the ambulance people dismissed them both and ran toward Zoe to save her. The Bride had to be saved first, so she'd look good in her wedding to the Beast.

Like all the other girls, Zoe was crying now. Each step she took toward the Ship of Light was a step away from Iris. It was just minutes before Zoe would vanish forever, and never be seen again. Cody and Colton managed to come over and grip Iris tight from both sides, in case she decided to do something crazy. Iris was paralyzed by fear and frustration. Whatever she did, no one was going to back her up. Colton and Cody weren't enough. Her father wasn't enough. The sovereign of the Beast needed an uprising. A great one, probably like the one that presumably happened in the past.

Zoe walked closer to the light, which was nothing but a great darkness. It was all about how you perceive things, Iris reminded herself. All you had to do is choose which side you were on. Man or Beast?

Zoe was going to see the Beasts' Pentimento. She was going to uncover the mystery. Sadly, whoever dug that deep never returned, so at least for now, the mystery would remain.

Why couldn't Iris just run to Zoe and face the Beast? Maybe because Colton and Cody were holding her still. Maybe because she feared the Council would hurt her dad. Maybe because Iris wasn't strong enough to risk being taken. But it wasn't that. It was because Iris believed she was more useful to Zoe staying down here in The Second.

Before Zoe was consumed by the light, she gazed back toward Iris. Like usual, the girls lowered their heads, as if Zoe was an epidemic. The Second was preparing themselves to forget a girl named Zoe existed. Iris stood tall, respecting her friend and nodding at her. Although

Cody was already sobbing next to Iris, he still held his head up high. Colton had to play strong to take care of Iris and his brother.

Zoe gazed at Cody, and blew him a kiss from her hand. Nothing else was going to happen between them. Then Zoe mouthed something to Iris. The same painful words Eva mouthed to her before. They were the same words. Ironic how the same words have a whole different impact, depending on whom the speaker is. The first time, Iris was shocked, but didn't truly respond to it. This time coming from Zoe, the mouthed words, "Avenge me," had an impact like no other.

35

Iris didn't eat. She didn't comb her hair and left it as stiff as it used to be when she was a kid. She didn't brush her teeth or change her clothes. If she could have taken off all her clothes and walked naked through the streets without embarrassing her dad, she would have done it.

Iris didn't speak to anyone. She had nothing to say, and her words would not have come out as sweet and polite. Her phone was locked. She slept the days away and cried silent tears at night, only getting out of bed to use the restroom. If it weren't for Charles feeding her, tolerating her, she might have starved to death by now.

Charles made sure no one saw her, not even Colton. His daughter needed to grieve, a situation hardly appreciated in The Second, as everyone had plastered happy smiles on their faces. At such a young age, grieving was like cutting through one's flesh with a razor. No human being should be grieving at seventeen. It was too early for such deep cuts.

Each day Iris came out of her room and asked her father if the Beasts had used their horn again. Her father told her "no." Then she would go back to her room, walking like a living zombie, and saying nothing.

Then one day, she opened the door and walked to her father who'd been reading. For the first time, she didn't ask about the Beasts. She was dressed to go out.

"What do you have in mind, Iris?" Charles asked calmly. "Is there anything I can do for you?"

"Did they catch the 'Beauty' yet?" she said, her eyes dry, void of moisture or light.

"Obviously not," Charles pointed at her and tried to sound playful.

"Are they still searching for me?"

"Every day," he said. "They never stop talking about the Beauty who gives roses to the Bride's parents. Why are you asking?"

Iris said nothing. She pulled out two roses from under her jacket. Actually, it was Colton's jacket, the one he'd left with her the night they kissed. Although unable to talk to Colton, she loved to feel its warmth on her.

Charles winced at the sight of the red roses. He'd never been a coward, but red roses had become officially illegal, a sign of the uprising. Teens who drew red roses on the walls of The Second were arrested and jailed by the law. Those were the teens who didn't know how to get a real red rose, because they didn't know anything about the Ruins. They only wanted to express their anger towards the Beasts. Iris was boldly holding two roses in her hand in the middle of the room.

"Where did you get those?" Charles said. "You haven't left the house in days."

"I realized I had kept two last roses in a vase under the bed." Iris said. "I hadn't watered them, but still...they refused to die."

"And here I thought you had some perfume sprayed in your room. What are you going to do with these roses, Iris?" Charles tried to choose his words carefully. He was torn between what he'd taught his daughter about the Pentimento, and her own safety she was risking by holding the roses.

"The roses always had a purpose, dad. One purpose." Iris said, her lips pale.

"You know you can't do this anymore," Charles shrugged. He'd taught her to do this, and now he was stopping her. A huge pet peeve of parenthood.

"I need you with me, dad." Iris wasn't bargaining. She had made up her mind in the time she'd spent alone in her room. "I can't do it alone. Please, dad."

"They will catch you, darling," Charles took off his glasses. He only called her "darling" when he needed to ask her favors. This time he was begging her to stay safe and not do it.

"So what? I'm no different than all the other Brides," she shrugged her shoulders.

"You are different. You're special, and ending up hurt by the Beasts won't help anyone."

"I owe this to my best friend, dad," Iris insisted. "You taught me that. You taught me about the Pentimento, that if I dig deep enough, I will eventually see through. You haven't taught me though what happens when I look deep enough and still don't see the truth. What do we do when we scratch the surface of the painting and still don't figure out what it was originally meant to be?"

"I don't know, Iris," Charles shrugged. "Any ideas?"

"We do what we only feel is right, dad. And I feel I need to honor my friend, so I can find a way to live with myself after her."

36

Charles stopped his car in front of Zoe's parents' house. Iris walked to the main door with the red rose in her hand. She turned around facing her father, and wrote her words on the snow: Zoe Peterson. You're not forgotten.

Iris stopped for a moment, reading the words she'd just written. She knelt down and signed it: the Beauty.

When standing up again, she read them one more time. She wasn't satisfied. "Beauty" was a term given to her by the Beasts. Standing up to them, she didn't want to use the name they had given her. Iris knelt down again. Wiped the snow clean, and signed: *Iris Charles Beaumont. No Beast's Beauty.*

Iris saw her dad fidget in his seat, worried someone would see them. She gave him a thumb's up, and turned around to ring the bell. Like always, once she pushed the button she would run back to her father's car. At least, this was what Charles was expecting.

Iris rang the bell and couldn't move. She stayed fixed in her place, waiting for Zoe's mother to open the door.

Charles began sweating. His daughter was exposing her cover deliberately.

"Sorry, dad." Iris mumbled, and felt the warm breeze from the house touch her face as Zoe's mother opened the door.

"Iris?" Zoe's mother didn't understand what was going on.

Iris raised the red rose to her. Zoe's mother's eyes widened, with unborn tears forming behind them. "It's you?" she said.

"Zoe deserves to be remembered," Iris said. "I'm not going to hide anymore. I wanted to let you know I'm barely going to live half a life without her next to me." Iris couldn't help it and threw herself in Zoe's mother's arms. The woman embraced her, unable to resist the tears anymore. This was a motherless child and daughterless mother, finding peace in each other's arms. Even Charles couldn't stop the tears from rolling down his cheeks while sitting in the driver's seat.

"I'm sorry the Beasts will arrest you now." Iris said. "Once they know you took the rose."

"It doesn't matter," the woman said. "Zoe deserves to be remembered. What about you, Iris? What are you going to do?"

"What I had to do from the beginning." Iris wiped her tears away. "Please tell my father I'm sorry too," she whispered, and turned away.

Iris ran into the dark of the streets, in the coldest of nights, away from everyone. It was a surprising move her father couldn't keep up with. She ran and ran, her heart pounding so hard, she thought it'd burst out of her rib cage and color the snow in red. Red as in red roses, the color the Beasts hate the most. Iris still had kept the other red rose in her jacket. Colton's jacket. She knew exactly where she was heading.

37

Once she slid Colton's father's card in the slot, the metallic door to the enormous Sinai tower opened. Iris dashed in, running toward the nearest elevator. On her way to it, she pushed the emergency button that would alert all police forces in The Second. It was showtime, but on her own terms.

She jumped into the elevator, pushed the button to the roof, and then picked up her phone. In a flash, she sent a message through all her networks; to Colton and Cody whose networks should spread the word to others too. It was a simple, yet unbelievable message: "I am on top of the Sinai tower."

She tapped her hands impatiently on the inner doors of the elevator until she reached the top. Stepping out into the cold, the wind slapped hard at her, as if trying to stop her from the insane thing she was about to do.

Iris stood in the middle of the rooftop, staring at the beautiful stars above. She craned her head up, wondering if she could glimpse the Beasts' ships beyond the stars.

"I know you're up there watching us, whoever you are." Iris shouted against the wind. "I know I am not crazy and I need you to respond back to me."

She got no reply but the wind swirling around her like a ghost. In the distance, she could see everyone in The Second waking up. She could hear the faint sound of the approaching police sirens. She'd managed to catch everyone's attention. Things were going as planned, except that no Beasts answered her from above.

"I know you're there," she said one more time, as she put her phone's camera on and connected it to a live feed on the internet, so everyone could see her breaking the rules by standing on top of the Sinai tower and challenging the Beasts to talk back to her. If they were actually up there. If they really existed. If they weren't an illusion. "I, Iris Beaumont, challenge the Beasts to take me as a Bride," she shouted.

The police force was closer now, probably in the elevators. She glanced at the news on her phone and saw everyone in The Second was broadcasting.

"You always pick one of us," she shouted at the sky full of stars. Those beautiful stars. "You never explain why. Don't you think we deserve to know why?" She took a deep breath. It was too late to back off now. "We're always afraid of you. We never get to see you, and yet you rule us, saying that taking one of us is for our own good. Now it's time one of us asks to be taken," she shouted from the top of her cold lungs. "I challenge you to take me as a Bride!"

The world gasped at Iris's request. In her mind, all she could think about was the Pentimento. Beyond this beautiful sky lay the truth about the Beasts. And if she couldn't figure it out here on Earth, then she'd better go to them, even if it were the end of her.

"Talk to me!" Iris shouted as the elevator doors opened, the police circling her with their laser guns pointed at her.

No one talked back to Iris. The sky was just as dark and dead as it always had been. But Iris wasn't going to give up. She made sure the reporters had arrived. Everyone was getting this on camera.

In a flash, Iris pulled out her last red rose and raised it in the sky. "Uprising!" she screamed, knowing the rose was the ultimate offense to the Beasts. It was the only thread to whatever happened in the past. It was the one thing that refused to die or grow ill in the Ruins. The perfect symbol against the Beasts.

"Please put down the rose," a police officer, pointing his red laser at her, asked her. "Possession of a red rose is against the law, miss."

Iris didn't care. She tiptoed, still holding the red rose.

"If you don't comply, miss, I will have to shoot you," the police officer warned her.

Iris knew she was out of options. She thought she'd try this last phrase to provoke the Beasts, "Humans only see what they...!" she shouted.

Even the police officer squinted at the strangeness of her sentence. "Don't shoot," another police officer said. "She could be insane. Maybe she needs medical treatment. Shoot her with a sedative."

Iris saw another officer aim at her. It was over. She must have been wrong. It was all in her head. There were no Beasts up there. All she could do was hold onto the rose, look up, and grit her teeth. "Take me as a Bride!"

Her last words echoed, as the police officer didn't pull the trigger to sedate her. Not because he'd changed his mind, but because of the massive light that shone suddenly down from the sky. It was blinding, as if an enormous pearl was looking down upon them on top of the Sinai tower.

Even Iris couldn't stand the light with its heat, melting the snow around her. All she knew was that this was the same light the Brides walked through. Iris took a brave deep breath, knowing it might be her last, at least on Earth, and stepped into the light. She was the first girl in history to walk into it willingly.

Whatever happened after Iris entered the light was beyond her perception. She felt like she was entering a dream while awake. Nothing made sense, and nothing quite lingered in her memory. This was a new world, so unlike The Second. How different? She had no idea.

All she could see was that glaring white light. It conjured blackness to her soul, blindness to her senses, and irony to her eyes.

She wondered if this was how it felt right before being exposed to the final Pentimento of things. Maybe in order to truly see anything, we had to experience a temporary blindness.

There was an enamoring scent of flowers in the distance. It compelled her to walk farther. Underneath her, the ground was getting colder. Marble floors, she thought. She lowered her head, but couldn't confirm her assumption. The floor must have been white. The greatest trick the Beasts ever pulled was imprisoning humans in the illusion of clarity. She wasn't even sure if anything she saw was real.

In the end, the flower smell turned out to be another devious trick of the Beasts. Its scent was definitely mesmerizing, but its effect was deception in a white dress. Iris's head felt heavy. The dizziness crawled up her veins and saturated her head. She ended up falling to her knees and then tumbled to one side, sleeping on the cold floor wherever she was. Before she totally lost consciousness, she thought she saw an endless number of stars underneath her.

Iris woke up in the middle of ugly monsters surrounding her. Her body trembled at their sight. She had never seen ugliness like this. Their features were so grotesque, her mind refused to even comprehend it. Ignorant to her surroundings, she was about to close her eyes and wish they'd just disappear. But she couldn't. The Beasts were closing in.

Weakened, she looked for a weapon around her, to protect herself. She found none. Was this how things would end, just like that, without explanations?

Dying seemed so miniature all of a sudden, compared with not knowing the truth.

She found that something had been tucked in her hand while she was asleep. A brush. A painter's brush, like the ones her dad used on the portraits when she was young.

Iris looked puzzled and wondered if the Beasts were still mocking her, controlling her dreams, and giving her a useless tool, instead of a knife or a gun to defend herself. What use was a brush or a pen in facing the evil in the world?

The Beasts trotted closer. They were slow and bent their backs like gorillas. It was as if walking on two legs was something new to them, something too evolutionary. They growled as if they didn't know the words, drummed their chest and drooled from between their sharpened teeth. Iris doubted the girls were really Brides. She leaned to the idea that they were food for the cannibalistic Beasts.

In her defense, Iris did the illogic, and waved the useless brush at them. Her last resort. Maybe the brush possessed magical powers. She certainly hoped so. But she was wrong. It wasn't an enchanted brush as she had hoped.

Something else happened though. Whenever she waved the brush in the air, a part of the world around her disappeared, as if she were holding a magical eraser, wiping away reality, and changing it into some white void.

She could not believe her eyes. This was insanity itself. As the Beasts closed in, insanity didn't seem like a bad option anymore. She bet she could use the brush on her predators. Brush them away, like a bad dream. Erase them the way historians demolished the truth about the past. Maybe the Beasts will disappear.

She took a deep breath and slashed the brush in the air as if it were a sword, and then...

40

Iris woke up panting from the dream. There were no Beasts nearby. In fact, she was in a place she'd never expected.

She found herself in a luxurious room that looked as if it were cut right out of fairy tale books, where she'd play princess and wait for her Prince Charming. A safe and enchanting place.

The room's ceiling was an enormous vault, engraved with writings and scriptures foreign to her world in The Second. They were beautiful. Otherworldly. Ancient, she guessed. The designs were like what she could have found in the Ruins before they'd been *ruined*. Everything exuded the feeling of time and significance. Things that had been created years and years ago, built by men and women who insinuated feelings and meanings into their creation. Nothing here was designed without reason.

Iris felt happy in her heart for a moment. The drawings looked as old as the core of the Earth, or the flames of the sun. The vault itself was about three stories high and showed the stars behind the inlaid glass on top.

This wasn't just a room. It was some kind of mansion in space.

Lowering her head, she saw all kinds of ornaments on the walls. Gold and blue were the dominant colors. The colors looked natural, unlike the metallic feel of The Second. Real organic paint. Everything looked as if crafted with keen hands. It almost looked as if it was made of some elegant clay, but it wasn't. The furniture and everything surrounding it was simply made by hand. No machinery was involved. Each piece of art showed slight flaws that men imprinted on things. That beautiful flaw that differentiates human from machine. It felt absurd to be experiencing humanity in the chamber of the Beasts.

Iris assumed the Beasts made the girls do the decorating and designs. Was this why most of them were talented?

Iris saw a window right in front of her. It looked upon a great wide blue sky, filled with stars as well. She craned her head forward to make sure. There were stars, real stars, right outside her window, twinkling like silver fireflies. Swinging slightly, as if hung with fine threads from a higher sky. They were beautiful.

There was a pool, the shape of a huge heart, separating her from the window. Its water was a mesh of beautiful light-green and blue. Golden feathers twinkled right above its surface. And a golden fish sprung out momentarily, then sank back again. She thought the fish were rather curious, peeking to see who she was.

Finally, Iris had to look at the bed she was now sitting upon. It was humongous, with four Corinthian columns on each corner. She knew they were Corinthian because she'd seen similar in the Ruins. A sign of how the world looked in The First.

All kinds of fine dresses were laid carefully around her. There was a basket of the finest fruits. She sat in the middle of the bed. If she wanted to get off of it, she had to crawl on all fours to reach the edge.

The sheets were as smooth as a baby's skin. Warm as a lover's embrace. They smelled of too many kinds of flowers. She doubted someone could stain them. How do you stain such beauty?

The dress she wore was beyond imaginable. Its texture reminded her of doves. It flowed, following the curves of her body religiously. It seemed designed for her specifically, made for her to wear at this very moment, respecting her exact weight and curves. It was a wedding dress.

But it was unlike any dress she had seen the Brides wear before. This one was designed by the Beasts.

Although this wasn't the place she'd imagined, Iris resisted the temptation. She wasn't impressed by it. All of this was to cover the Beasts' ugliness, maybe their weaknesses.

Iris crawled out of bed and continued inspecting the room. The drawers were filled with all kinds of perfumes with unearthly scents--just like the one that sedated her, she thought.

The wardrobes were filled with dresses, shoes, and jewelry. They weren't really wardrobes. They were long rooms. She couldn't help but check the cloth, touch it, and feel it on her cheeks. Everything was perfectly her size. All White. Things that she might have enjoyed on Earth. She snapped out of her stupor, and abandoned the wardrobes back to the chamber. The temptations were high, but was the price even higher?

Focusing, she saw there was no way out of the chamber. There were no doors. Only that window behind the pool. It looked locked. She wasn't going to open a window overlooking the stars. Would she be able to even breathe if she did? Where do you escape to when you're locked in space?

She looked around one last time and understood what this beautiful chamber was. Her prison. She wondered if she was part of the Beasts' harem, called whenever they desired her.

"Hello?" she called to the nothingness. She made sure her voice wasn't smeared with the slightest intimidation. Although afraid, she had to pose as an opponent. She was unlike other Brides, and was going to demand not to be treated like one. She asked to be here. That should count.

Still, when a secret door opened from the walls, she winced and took a step back.

41

Someone, covered in a white veil from head to toe, entered the room. The veil was made from an unearthly cloth, but wasn't transparent. It made the intruder look like a ghost, except that Iris could see the bare feet and hands of a girl, probably her age.

"Did you sleep well?" the ghost girl asked. She sounded friendly and surprisingly caring.

Iris nodded, wishing the girl wouldn't come any closer. She watched her do so though, handing her a warm towel she'd been holding.

"Rub this on your face," the girl offered. "It will refresh you, and remove any trace of the poison you drank."

"Poison?"

"Don't worry. It's not as scary as it sounds. We call all sedatives poison here. Most girls need them in the beginning, until they stop resisting."

"Resisting what?"

"That this is your fate and that it isn't a bad thing," the girl stretched her arms further, offering the steaming towel.

Iris took the towel and rubbed her face. It smelled of lilies and it made her actually feel good.

"Rub it on your eyes too." The girl suggested. "It will help you see better."

Reluctantly, Iris did. She actually felt her irises relax. Something strange was happening to her eyes. Things were blurry at first, but then she saw again. This time she noticed everything around her looked a bit sharper, and even more beautiful.

"What kind of fate are we talking about?" Iris had to ask, forgetting about all these temptations. "If only one's fate was that predictable, it wouldn't have been called 'fate,'" the girl said.

Iris thought she sounded as if she were smiling. If only she'd remove the veil, so Iris could see her face.

"I'm not sure I understand what this means." Iris said.

"Fate isn't an open book. It's a mystery, and I'd hate to spoil it for you," the girl said politely.

"I don't mind if you spoil mine, believe me."

"No. You do mind. You just don't know it," the girl insisted.

Iris didn't know how to argue with such nonsense.

"Are you a Bride?" she wondered.

"I'm your servant," the girl said. "I am here to take care of you, until you meet your Master."

"My Master?"

"Each girl is chosen by one of the honorable Masters here," the girl explained.

"You mean the Beasts." Iris wasn't asking. Of course, the Beasts thought of themselves as Masters. She wouldn't be surprised if they thought of themselves as beautiful too.

"An Earthly description that's unwelcome here," the girl said. "My Masters are no Beasts. Humans made that name up. My Masters would appreciate it if you don't call them such names," the girl said.

"So *My Master* alien would like to see me? Huh?" Iris said.

The girl was silent for a moment. Iris could sense a slight anger behind the veil. "My Masters are no aliens either," she said. Her loyalty to the Beasts was puzzling.

"They are Masters of the New World."

"The New World?" Iris wondered.

The girl didn't reply. It was a useless discussion with someone Iris couldn't even see anyways. She wouldn't be surprised if the girl was a Beast herself. There was no point in debating.

"It'd be a good idea if I leave you a couple of minutes to clear your mind, before meeting your Master," the girl said, bowing even lower now. "Your Master doesn't like Brides with unclear minds. He has a special fascination with the human mind. Women's especially."

"That's shocking for someone who collects random Brides." Iris almost laughed.

"Master Andre has a special liking for you," the girl added.

"Master Andre?" Iris chewed on the words. The Beasts had names? Human names? As if this would change who they really were.

"He is also fascinated with eyes," the girl went on. "I heard him say funny things about yours," the girl snickered from underneath the veil.

"My eyes?"

"He's fascinated with them. Master Andre believes in you. He defied many of his family's rules for you. After all, you are the girl who raised the red rose in their faces. You challenged them and came willingly. For thousands of years, I haven't seen this before. Other Masters bid to have you."

"They bid for me?" Iris felt offended. She was practically a slave for the highest price. And to worsen it, she was bid on by aliens.

"They never tell us how they bid, but Master Andre, a young respectable prince, won you," she said.

"Should I feel special?" Iris pursed her lips. If she didn't like this place and its logic, then it was all her fault. She was the one that asked to be here. "Did you say prince?"

"Yes, he is."

Iris decided she wasn't going to comment on this part. A prince of Beasts was the last thing she needed in her life...or the few days left of it.

"Tell me. Did you hear anything about a girl named Zoe?" Iris said.

"Of course," the girl nodded. "The last Bride taken before you."

"Can you tell me anything about her? Do you know where she is? Is she alive?"

"I am afraid I'm not authorized to say," the girl said. "And it'd be better if you don't ask. It could get you in trouble, My Beauty. Now, I have to leave, and will be back when your mind clears."

"My mind is clear right now," Iris challenged her. "Take me to this Andre, now."

"No, your mind isn't clear yet, My Beauty," the girl said. "The towel's effect takes some time."

"This towel is supposed to clear my mind?"

The girl nodded.

"What do you mean by that? I'm telling you, my mind is alert and clear. How would you know me better than I know myself?"

The girl paused. Iris sensed the girl wanted to tell her something, but couldn't bring herself to it. "Have you seen the magnificent stars outside your window, My Beauty?" the girl said irrelevantly.

Iris blinked at the absurd question. "Yes. I saw them when I was down on Earth too. What about them?"

"What do they look like?"

"What? They look like stars!" Iris snapped.

"Just stars?"

"Are you playing games with me?" Iris said. "Take me to your Master, now."

"I can't," the girl said. "Not unless you see the stars. A sign that your mind has cleared. Now, I'd like to excuse myself and come back in a while. I'm sure the towel's effect should grow on you by then."

The girl walked out, still paying her respects by bowing her head. The door she left from turned into a wall right after her.

42

Things were getting weirder for Iris. Instead of expecting to deal with a monster Beast, she was treated like some kind of princess in a kingdom in space. To top it off, she was supposed to do things like "clear her mind," whatever that meant.

She should have tried to catch the door in the wall while it was still open, and escape the room.

All Iris wanted was to look for Zoe and save her like heroes do in books. Then again, she knew it was impossible. Iris challenged the Beasts to know what was going on. It was unlikely they'd just let her save Zoe. She needed to act smoothly, and see what this place was exactly.

The bed's sheets felt fine as she sat on them again, staring at the window with the stars. What was she supposed to do now, stare at the stars and see?

Crap.

The Beasts still liked games. They loved mocking her, and messing with her mind. She was sure these were stars outside her window, the same beautiful stars she'd tried to catch when standing atop of the Sinai tower.

She didn't know why, but she gave it a try. She rubbed her eyes and looked again. The stars looked a little blurry, that's all, until her eyes cleared again. Her mind didn't "clear," though. The girl was talking nonsense.

Iris stepped down into the pool of faint green and sparkling blue and plodded forward. The water was warm, relaxing, as if to hypnotize her before reaching the window. She let the sparkling gold feathers gather on her dress and face. They felt like sunrise on her skin. The fish weren't harmful, as they tickled her feet below. Things were too beautiful in this pool, it almost seemed unreal.

What did you expect, Iris? The Beasts are the Gods of our world. They have everything; power and money, and they live in the clouds. They are magicians. They can create worlds, destroy worlds, and control humans. Things had to be this beautiful up here, because it all compensates for the one thing they lack: Beauty.

Iris reached the window and stuck her nose to it. What she was looking at were still stars.

She pressed her hands against the glass, remembering Colton all of a sudden. Maybe it was the sense that Colton was down there somewhere on Earth, just beyond the stars. Did she sacrifice his love for her best friend? Since no Bride ever returned, it seemed unlikely that she'd see him again. She hadn't even consulted him or her father about it. But they'd have stopped her. It was an impulsive move in many ways, but she had acted out of anger and passion for her friend. Hell, she was afraid she'd be taken sooner or later. She had to do something about it and the price was breaking Colton's heart, which was in many ways, hers too.

Iris turned away from the window, wondering if being here had been her fate from the beginning, like the girl in white said. From the first day she wished Eva would be taken by the Beasts, then Eva asking her to avenge her, and then the Beasts taking Zoe. Ending up here felt like the natural process of events. If there was a wisdom behind this fate, she couldn't tell what it was.

The door opened behind her again.

"I see you enjoyed your bath, My Beauty," the girl said, offering her a robe as Iris stepped out of the water. "Did your mind clear?"

Iris let the girl cover her with the robe. "I don't think so," she pursed her lips. "I still see stars outside my window."

"Don't worry," the girl said. "It happens. Sooner or later, your mind will clear. Master Andre decided to see you, even if your mind hasn't cleared yet. He is eager to meet you," she snickered again.

"So, shall we?" Iris said, all wet and clumsy.

"Right after I wash you, and dress you properly for your Master, My Beauty," the girl said.

43

The hallway behind the door was all white with faint lights. The floor beneath her feet was made of glass, overlooking the stars. She let out a shattered sigh for a moment. Part of it was fearing she'd fall into the oblivion of space underneath; she was practically staring at the universe from above. Another part was that she was enchanted by the beauty of what she saw.

The ugly Beasts were enjoying this magnificent view of the world from above every day. Far away, beyond the stars beneath her feet, Iris could see the Earth. Although she couldn't make out the details, it was a fabulous scene. Where she came from was the most beautiful and enchanting painting she had ever seen. It was just like she'd always imagined it would be. Almost the same way she pictured it in school, and how everyone thought the Earth looked from above.

The ghost girl stopped Iris before a white wall. Iris watched her hum indecipherable words from underneath the veil, until the wall turned into another door. The girl bowed, showing her the way into another large chamber.

It was as beautiful as her room. The same vaulted ceiling, a pool, and windows to the stars. But it was a bit more majestic, like a prince's suite. Iris felt bewilderment, smelling the red rose's scent filling the room. The very same forbidden flower. How could it be?

"Please sit, My Beauty," the girl ushered her to the long dining table with one chair at each end. Her chair looked like a throne. She noticed another semi-transparent veil draped down onto the middle of the table, separating her from whomever was going to sit on the other side. Master Andre, she supposed.

Iris cupped the sides of her dress and enjoyed pretending to be in fairy tale, expect this one would be a fairy tale of lies.

Sitting on the throne filled her with that unexplainable feeling of power. It was as if she was slowly sympathizing with those who held great power in their hands. It felt so good, and giving it up was impossible. How would you give up being a God?

The girl excused herself and left the room. Iris sat silently, looking at the thin veil, separating her from whomever was going to share this endless amount of food and wine on the table with her.

The Beasts must be so ugly, her Master couldn't bring himself to expose his looks to her.

The waiting was uncomfortable for her, but she registered that life in this place was slow by default. No one seemed rushed. They took their time. And why not? They were the rulers of the world. There was no parent rushing them to wake up and go to school, no job they'd be fired from upon a late arrival, and most importantly, there was no one they feared or sought to please. It occurred to Iris that fear actually moved the world on Earth.

Historians would say it was love that moved the world, but they were lying. Every move down there was out of fear. Fear of arriving late, fearing of not being able to perform a task, fear of being left behind, dying alone, not being loved. As a girl, the most imminent fear right now was being taken further into the unknown.

A long breath filled her lungs with the rose-scented air. She needed it. She closed her eyes for a moment, she needed to keep pretending she was brave enough to face the Beast.

Opening her eyes again, she caught a glimpse of the Beast's shadow sitting on the other side of the table behind the curtain.

44

It was like a silhouette of a tall man. His figure was tight and athletic, but she couldn't tell more. He definitely had long hair that fluttered down his shoulders. His presence, even behind the curtain, was unavoidable. It was as if the world disappeared around her when he half-showed up. He was one of the rulers of the world, Iris thought. She wouldn't have expected a lesser impact from him.

"Have you had a good sleep?" he inquired. His voice was young, raw, and low, as if it resonated straight from his chest. Authoritative. A voice that demanded answers without saying it.

"I did." Iris said. All of her inquiries escaped her momentarily. Was she supposed to say something like, "Yes, my prince?" His presence still baffled her. She wasn't here to become an obeying Bride. She was here to see. Yes, see right through the Beasts' Pentimento. Not see through the silly stars, like the girl asked of her. "Everyone seems overly concerned about me having slept well," she mumbled, stabbing the meat in front of her with her fork. A fake smile colored her face afterwards.

"Sleep is crucial to the mind." He had heard her, which wasn't a big deal. She wondered if Beasts possessed otherworldly powers. Could he read her mind? Why is everyone talking about seeing and the mind since she arrived to this ship of light? Was that how the Beasts ruled, reading humans like an open book? Or was it what they needed to study?

"Is that what you're after, the human mind?" Iris said, trying to sound more polite than she had ever been before.

"The human mind is fascinating," the Beast said. She wasn't comfortable with thinking of him as Master Andre yet. "And yet a terrible thing," he added.

"That didn't answer my question," Iris said. "Are you after our minds?"

"What difference does it make if we are?" the Beast said.

"Because if so, you got it all wrong," Iris said. "It's here that makes us unique," she pointed at her heart.

The Beast stayed silent for a while. She wished she could see the expression on his face right now. But she was sure he didn't eat or move his head for a while. He instead kept looking towards her, she supposed. Her words must have strummed a high note. "As I said, sleep is very crucial to the human mind."

"Sleep again, huh." Iris felt stronger for a moment. He escaped the conversation. Pressed the rewind button in his alien mind and started all over again, like a clean slate. How typical of an alien. She wondered if he was programmed through a chip in his ugly brain. Was he capable of traveling through time?

"How could you tell reality from dreams, if you don't get a dose of healthy dreams while sleeping?" he began eating again, Iris saw from the movement of his silhouette behind the curtain or veil, or whatever that thin barrier was. He ate with bare hands and teeth, grabbing what looked like a turkey's thigh in his grip and sinking his face into it. Iris shrugged. Hunger like that was the first sign of bestiality. She lowered her head to the meat in front of her and wondered if it was human. Bridal, maybe?

"So what is actually real, and what is a dream?" She was making silly conversation to stop her heart from speeding up.

Her Master stopped in the middle of a bite, and lowered his turkey to the plate. He pulled a napkin and wiped his mouth. He did it elegantly. He was a pool of contradicting behaviors.

"That's the first time I've been asked such questions by a Bride," he laughed. A confident laugh; neither scary, nor safe.

"I'd say you have to get used to it." Iris shot back, trying not to sweat.

"I wouldn't expect lesser from a girl who came here willingly," he tilted his head. Iris wondered if he actually saw her vividly from behind the curtain. Was it possible it was a two-way mystery? Maybe the Beasts didn't know that much about humans. Maybe they saw them as ugly, like Cody had told Zoe. Like a painter giving way to the brushes in his hands to draw the most compelling portrait, then lying to his audience, saying he'd done every detail intentionally. "Let's start with you. What do you think tells a dream from reality?" he asked.

"Dreams are mostly lies," Iris said off the top of her head. She never believed in the sleeping dreams. Daydreaming was called "hope" in her book. "Therefore reality is simply..."

"Truth," he considered, lacing his hands before what looked like his chin. He looked like a chess master, waiting for his opponent's next move.

Iris nodded, not fond of him interrupting her. Hell, she wasn't sure why she was still talking to him. She could just jump over and pull the curtain. Curiosity was killing her.

"Which will lead us to the ultimate debate," he said. "What is really considered 'truth?'"

"Truth is as clear as the sun," she almost sneered at him. "Once you pull the curtain before your eyes." She heard him let out a low groan. He'd gotten the message and was mocking her attempt to provoke him.

"'Once you pull the curtain before your eyes,'" he whispered, quoting her. "Eyes," he repeated. "Just like your name, Iris," he leaned forward, just a little. And for the first time she could see something was glittering behind the curtain. It was probably his eyes. They were a golden shade of green, like nothing she'd ever seen before. Again, neither scary, nor safe. "Do you judge everything through your eyes, Iris?" He said it as if it were "eye-ris." "Is seeing the only road to believing in your book?"

"I wasn't given a pair of pupils for nothing." She didn't like the way he began cornering her in the conversation. She wasn't supposed to talk with Beasts. She was here to challenge them. "Unless you're ugly." She pressed her expensive shoes against the floor and gripped the dinner knife. "You'd prefer not to use your eyes in your judgment." Suddenly, she wasn't comfortable with his green eyes. She decided they leaned more toward being scary.

45

Master Andre didn't look offended. At least, no part of his silhouette showed it. He didn't say anything for a long time. The more his silence filled the room, the weaker Iris's grip felt on the knife, and on her own life. She let go finally. The Beast's calmness puzzled her and stripped her of all anger. To cover her weakness, she began eating again, not with her hands, but with a golden fork and spoon.

"I hope you like our food," he leaned back and began eating as well. "It's fresh, healthy, and tastes..."

"Unearthly?" she couldn't hold her tongue. It was a deserved pun. The food was devilishly delicious and she couldn't help but gorge on it. She told herself that she needed strength so she didn't feel guilty eating what she'd previously suspected to be human meat. Of course, it wasn't. Humans wouldn't taste so good.

"An older Master once told me that dreams are whatever you can escape by waking up," the Master said. "Truth, on the other hand, sticks to your soul. You can't wake up from it. That's why we need to dream actually, so we can balance our psyche."

You say *we* as if you are human," Iris noted.

"Maybe I was, once," he said, and finally she thought this was some kind of a hint. "Maybe I will be again." He destroyed all assumptions, and she couldn't help but think he was playing her.

Nothing was said for a while.

The sound of their chewing was painful to Iris's ears. She wasn't here to dine, yet there was nothing else she could do--and this damn food was irresistible. Iris suddenly forced herself to stop eating. She remembered the rose's scent. The food could be as devious. It might have an effect on her. "So is this what you do with all your Brides? Talk?" Iris slammed the knife back on the table. She was aware of her contradicting behavior, and it was alarming. Maybe she wasn't up to coming here willingly. The Beasts' presence was stronger than she'd imagined.

"You don't like talking?" Andre said.

"Not with someone I can't see."

"I'm not sure you're ready to see me yet," he explained, with no hint of embarrassment.

Iris felt this strange sympathy toward him again, and it felt so wrong. But her Master's acknowledgment of his ugliness was far from monstrous. She sensed his misery in a most unusual way. *I am so not myself today. What is happening to me? Did the towel do something to me?*

"Are you very ugly?" she shrugged enough to feel a lump of air in her throat.

"What's the difference between ugly and very ugly?" he sipped his soup calmly.

Those questioning answers again, Iris. Is he messing with your mind intentionally, or is he just humble and hurt?

"I don't know." She gave up. Since she'd arrived, no one fought with her or resisted her, lowering all her defenses. *How could you fight a Beast when he is not attacking you? And if he's not attacking you, should he still be considered a Beast?*

"I don't mind looking at you, whatever you look like," curiosity was eating her alive.

"I don't mind looking at you either," another puzzling answer.

"So you know what I look like. You can see me clearly from behind the veil," she was making a statement.

"Oh, I know what you look like," he laughed. His laugh made her tremble. It was loud and hollow. Too confident. Too bossy. Suddenly, she understood her confusion. It was his contradictions that confused her. He ate like a monster, then wiped his mouth elegantly with a napkin. What kind of species did that? "I, and my fellow Masters, have seen you challenge us with the red rose in your hand. That was quite a show."

"Was that funny to you?" she squinted.

"Funny?" he seemed to think it over. "No. It was admirable. That's why I haven't treated you like other Brides."

Iris heart sank into her belly. "What is it you do to other Brides?" she stood up. He did not fidget. "Do you hurt them?" He continued sipping his soup. Iris took a step forward, pondering the thought of attacking him. "What did you do to Zoe?"

The doors sprang open and the ghost girls entered. They held metallic rods with red lights in their hands.

The Master signaled them to a stop, standing up. He threw his napkin on the table and walked closer to the curtain. "I said you're not ready to see my face," he said firmly. "I like my words respected and honored. But I understand this is a new environment for you. You're away from home, and you're never going back. It takes time to believe it and cope with it, so I will forgive your misbehavior."

"You're in no position to forgive me," Iris's cheekbones tensed. "I'm not a Bride. I came here on my own." She heard the girls in white sigh and lower their heads, afraid she'd angered their Master.

The Beast took a moment again, before speaking. Secretly, she couldn't help but admire his stable posture and the silences he cherished before uttering a word. It was as if every word had to be calculated. Every word meant something, and he made sure it did. She saw him tap his fingers slightly on the table. "I'd prefer we end our dinner now. I like my Bride to be in a good mood."

Iris was going to object, but she was silenced by the warning hand he raised up in the air. She felt the urge to stop instantly. He wasn't fighting with her. He wasn't rude. And he didn't look like he was going to hurt her--at least, not now. His behavior made her snapping look ridiculous, even to herself.

"I advise you to go back to your chamber and clear your mind, then stare at the stars," he followed.

Clear my head and look at the stars, Iris thought. All this nonsense again. She stood silent as the girls circled her, and were about to drag her back to her chamber.

"I will see you again in a few thousand heartbeats," he said.

"Heartbeats?"

"We measure time by heartbeats here," he explained. "Because we cherish every moment in life. By a few thousand, I mean about four to five hours. I'd like to continue this conversation later."

"If you say so," Iris said. It was hard to tell if she was still playing fair until she learned enough about the Beast to find Zoe, or if she was really complying. She'd always been fascinated with Colton's personality, but this supposedly young and ugly prince exuded a calmness and grip over the situation like she'd never felt before. It was silly and unacceptable, thinking about him this way. Whatever they had sedated her with must have messed with her emotions. Iris gave in to the girls in white as they escorted her to the door.

"One more thing, Iris," Master Andre said before she left. "You need to know something before we meet again."

"I can't imagine what that might be," she said flatly, pretending she wasn't impressed with his personality.

"We have some sort of a list we use in choosing our Brides," he said.

"How sick of you," she said.

"It's a very delicate list," he continued. "Each Bride has been chosen very carefully, in ways you could not imagine."

"Why are you telling me this?"

"Because next week's Bride was going to be you," he said. "I thought you should know, so we can get over this part about you challenging us. Your actions were daring and immensely admirably by the Masters, but let's just be open about the fact that I was going to have you next week, no matter what."

"Is that why you're treating me unlike other Brides?" Iris shrugged. "Because, according to your schedule, my time has not come?"

Silence again, for about a hundred heartbeats. "I'm still trying to figure that out." Master Andre said.

46

Back through the hallway, the girls escorted Iris toward her room. She didn't know why, but she stared at the stars beneath her feet again. Something felt so out of place. She wished she could figure it out.

Even though the girls were many, she seriously thought about escaping them to explore the ship. How hard could it be? She'd been escaping the android guards at school for a long time. She let the girls walk her as she glanced over, trying to see anything that made sense. There was nothing. All white walls, all the way. If she was going to escape, she needed a direction to run to and hide.

Where are you Cody? She thought. Would he have a way to hack the Beasts?

A silver device in one of the girls' hands beeped. The girl held it up at eye-level and closed her eyes. She looked as though she was listening to something Iris couldn't hear. "I'll do as you please, My Master," she said, and clicked the device's button. Iris believed it to be some kind of cellular. One that worked on the mind.

"Master Andre wants you to see something," the girl told Iris. "He says you will like it, and it will help you clear your mind."

"I doubt I will like it," Iris said, then wished she hadn't. What was wrong with going somewhere else and exploring more of the ship. "On second thought, why not?" she smiled.

"As you wish, My Beauty," the girl bowed and told the others to leave them, then ushered Iris to another room. The door opened with the same technique; the girl whispered to it, and it opened. Everything in this ship seemed to work with the power of the mind.

"Please," the girl showed her into a new chamber.

This one was a bit darker. It reminded her of her father's basement, full of paintings, brushes, portraits, and tables to draw on. It took Iris a moment to realize this was a painter's studio. And she understood why Andre thought she'd like it. This was where she could practice her most desired hobby, the one that made her question everything around her, and brought her here.

"I do like it," Iris said. She couldn't deny it. It was from the heart. The place was filled with instruments and chemicals used in her dad's Pentimento studio. It reminded her of her family and her childhood.

Her curiosity urged her to explore the paintings, until she came upon Fragonard's *Fountain of Love*. Iris stood inanimate before it for a while, wondering if this was a copy or some kind of fake. Did Fragonard paint another one, or did the Beasts steal it from her father? If yes, when did they do that? She remembered last seeing it two days ago.

Iris pulled the painting toward a black light nearby and looked through, wondering if she'd see the boy was really a beast. She saw it. The boy had been designed as a beast in the beginning and then changed. It was either her father's copy, or the same painting.

"I told you." Andre appeared from behind a painting. He was wearing a white veil, just like the girl. Only this one was embroiled with golden stripes. Andre looked a bit taller now, standing only strides away.

"I thought you said you wanted to continue the conversation later." Iris said, as the girl excused herself out.

"I still do," Andre walked around her. He smelled of red roses. She wondered why he wore a veil, making him look like a ghost. Couldn't the Beasts invent a technology that would make them disappear and become only sounds or something? "This is something entirely different," he followed.

"Do you even know what this place is, or did you just steal my father's paintings?" Iris sneered.

"We didn't steal anything," Andre said. "This Fragonard painting has been here for ages."

"How can you say that? My father discovered the Pentimento underneath it. The boy was originally a beast. You're lying."

"No, it's been here since long ago," Andre insisted. "We've been studying it, and interpreting its hidden messages since long ago. Aren't you curious about the message?"

"There is a message?" Iris's eyes moistened. She'd been waiting to know why the boy was a beast for most of her life. Although she assumed Andre was lying to her, she couldn't resist listening to him about the real meaning behind the painting.

"A message about the future, yes," Andre said. "In this case, Fragonard's future, which is the 'now' for us."

"What is it? Was he trying to warn us about you?" Iris stepped forward. "Do you Beasts look like the Beast boy hidden beneath his painting?"

"Pentimento is an old art," Andre said, walking away from her, checking out some of the other paintings, discarding her questions. "I like to work here for hours. It clears my mind in so many ways."

She wasn't going to comment on the "clearing his mind" part. And she wasn't going to push for answers she knew weren't easy to get. Seriously, she had enough. She was rather interested in an ugly Beast who practiced Pentimento. She had to stick around until he spilled out the truth. Iris needed to find the Beast's weakness.

"Are you trying to convince me you actually practice this art?" Iris said.

"Why would you doubt that? Because I'm ugly?"

"Why? Are you kidding me? It's prohibited by the Beasts. If you practice it, how can you make it illegal on Earth?"

"It's a bit too soon to talk about that," Andre considered. "I was hoping you'd ask me something else."

"Like what?" Iris sighed.

"Like what I like about it. Why I do it." He had a point, Iris thought. She let him continue. He sounded passionate about it. "When I was a kid, an old Master once told me a peculiar story about the continent of America when it was first discovered."

"America? You mean The First United States of America?" She found herself asking one question after another, clueless to Andre's vague stories, and his habit of answer a question with a question--or some other irrelevant story.

"It wasn't called The First at the time. It's a name humans made up later. But if you prefer to call it that, be my guest," he nodded.

"Okay. What about America?"

"America was originally inhabited by Red Indians, the original locals of the land, a very, very long time ago," Andre laced his hands behind his back as he circled her. He wore white gloves, so she couldn't see his hands.

"Then a man called Christopher Columbus, if I remember right, discovered it by chance, as he sailed across the oceans."

"Really?" Iris thought Cody, Colton, and Zoe would like to hear this story, if they were here. This was a story about The First before it became The Second, a story told by the Beasts, who ruled the world and owned the key and knowledge to what really happened in the past. "I've never heard this before. Go on." She welcomed his story.

"The Indians were a primitive nation. They lived in tents called 'teepees,' and ate directly from the products of the earth. They loved their lives as they were, and thought that was all there was. Never had they even pondered the thought of sailing the ocean and discovering the world beyond the tides. The ocean was their world's end," Andre said. "But then, when Columbus first arrived in his ships, something incredibly unexpected happened."

Iris was all ears, all eyes, with heart and soul. There was nothing more exciting than knowing who her ancestors were. That's why her father had taught her the Pentimento, in hopes to know who they really were someday. Why Andre lied about the Fragonard being in their possession all this time, still didn't make sense. "What happened?" she wondered.

"Are you sure you can handle it?" Andre said. "Because you need a really clear mind to imagine it."

"Enough with the clear mind thing," she said. "I am a big girl. I am handling you. Tell me the story."

"Alright," Andre said. "What happened is that the Red Indians didn't see the ships."

"Are you kidding me? The ships sailing the ocean must have been huge. Ah, you mean Columbus had some kind of technology that could make these ships invisible, right?"

Andre laughed. Iris didn't like anyone laughing at her. "There were no such technologies in their time," he said. "But still, the Indians didn't see the ships with their eyes at first glance," Andre said. "It happened later, when one of them saw the ships and told the others there was something in the water. He thought it was a creature of the sea with wings and that it was far away, but was getting bigger and bigger."

"What kind of nonsense is that?"

"It's not nonsense," Andre said. "It's how the mind works. The Indians had never seen a ship. They had never even been exposed to the idea that a ship existed. The idea of sailing in the sea was utter madness to them, and they had never been introduced to it. So think of it this way: the Indians' minds saw a certain reality in front of them, a reality that their mind had not been introduced to before. So what do you think the mind does to a human when challenged this way?"

Iris felt dizzy, but she liked the story. It was hard to fully comprehend, but she could relate to it, not understanding why. A strange feeling overwhelmed her briefly. "What does this story have to do with you practicing the Pentimento?" she asked.

"This story was the first time I was introduced to the idea of Pentimento," Andre explained.

"But Pentimento is only a painter's term."

"That's where you and I, and your father probably, differ," Andre said. "The ships the Indians couldn't see was a Pentimento of sorts. In fact, there are all kinds of Pentimentos in this world. When you look at a flower that reminds you of someone and it takes you back to an old memory deep inside you, that's Pentimento. When a photograph reminds you of how you felt in a certain moment, that's Pentimento. And when you neglect someone's looks for a moment and learn about them, talk to them, and share experiences with them--a moment when you see their true beauty, that's Pentimento."

Iris suddenly wanted to leave the room and go back to her chamber. It had only been an hour or so, and Andre's conversation made her feel an unexplainable, unreasonable, an almost inhuman attraction to him. It was so wrong, she could not understand it. The only way to accept it was to believe the words he'd just said; to forget he was a Beast, that he was ugly, a monster, and unrighteously took girls from her world.

The thought made her want to see his face right now. She needed to lose her interest and attraction right now, and she thought seeing his beastly face would solve that for her.

She was in love with Colton. And although she might not see him again, it didn't mean she'd stop loving him.

But Andre not only shared her hobby; he understood it, even deeper than she thought he did. He understood her need to know, to explore. He was a beast with a heart of an artist. He was dominant, grounded, and passionate about what he loved. And she'd learned all of this about him within an hour. An hour of talking, not seeing his face. Andre was like an ugly rock, sitting solid by the shore, content with what it is, and all Iris needed was to crash into him like a foolish tide.

"Do you understand me?" Andre repeated. All she could do was raise her eyes back to him. Her lips were sealed, her mind wandering, and her heart thudding. "Pentimento actually describes the human condition. People are made of layers upon layers. Somewhere in that deepest layer lies the true self, what they were meant to be in the first place. Some stay true and surface with a layer that is no different than the deepest one, and some lose their way and become something else."

Iris shrugged. She felt numb, and again, she didn't know why. She was being lectured by a Beast about humanity and it puzzled her how they saw right through them. "Is that Picasso?" she changed the subject, trying to silence the emotion buzzing in her mind.

"It is," Andre pointed at a painting on the table. "The Old Guitarist, one of the most famous Pentimentos in the world. What we see and what he'd painted initially are two different things."

"Did he have as message as well?" Iris inquired reluctantly.

"I don't really know." Andre said.

"Strange. Aren't you are a Beast? I mean, a Master? You must know everything."

"We know what we've had a chance to interpret or investigate. But generally, you could say we've arrived too late," he explained. "The world was already destroyed."

"Was is that bad?"

For the first time, Andre lowered his head behind the veil. She couldn't tell if it was guilt, empathy, or respect. "Like many other things, let's not talk about this now," he said. "I wanted you to see this room and maybe explore the many paintings I have here. I thought it would make you happier, and help us continue the conversation later today."

"The one about Zoe," Iris insisted. "Are you going to tell me what happened to Zoe?"

"Shouldn't you be worried about what's going to happen to you?" he said.

Iris shrugged, hoping this wasn't a threat. The Beast, who called himself Prince Andre, was half-disappearing into whatever invisible door he'd come from. His veil was half white, half dark now. A perfect analogy to how she felt about him, about what he really was, and how Iris perceived every word he said.

"I'll leave you with your artistic hobby," Andre said. "Enjoy it, until we meet again in a few thousand heartbeats. I believe we'll have a much better conversation, and I promise I will answer some questions. Until your time comes, we have a lot to talk about."

"Prince Andre!" Iris said, before he disappeared. Calling him prince was her feeble tactic, until she knew what he wanted to do to her later, when her time came. What an uncomfortable thought.

"Yes, Iris?" he said, without turning around.

"Was it really horrible what happened to the world before you came?" she wondered.

"Did you ever ask yourself why your nation is called The Second?" Like usual, he answered with a question.

"Should I?" she thought she'd play his game.

"We called you The Second because after what you had done to the world, we wanted to give you a second chance."

47

Back in her chamber, Iris asked her servant girl to show her around, so she could enjoy everything in it. Iris's plan was to learn as much as possible from her about the Beast's world. The girl was honored to help her princess. Still, in the middle of all of this, she offered Iris another towel to clear her mind.

"Aren't you going to tell me what I am supposed to see or hear with this towel?" Iris befriended her.

"Of all things, this is one of the things I am most not allowed to discuss with you, My Beauty," she said. "I am afraid I don't really know what you're supposed to see."

"Don't you have a clear mind yourself?"

"I do. Very much," she said. "And if I don't, the Masters help me restore clarity. They taught me meditation."

"Meditation?" Iris nodded. "So if you don't mind me asking, did you live in The Second before?"

"I also can't say, My Beauty," the girl stowed some of the dresses in the closet. "Would you like me to give you a massage?"

"Sounds like a great idea." Iris pretended to be interested.

"As you wish, My Beauty. Just lay on your stomach," the girl showed her to a special bed in the chamber. It was fixed right above a glassy part where she could see the stars below her, just like in the hallways. Iris felt reluctant as she took her dress off.

"Don't worry, My Beauty," the girl said. "You will not fall back down to Earth," she laughed. "The glass is stronger than steel. And it's a nice view to the stars, while enjoying your massage."

Iris gave in eventually and got on the bed. The view was dreamy and the girl's hands were just the right pressure. It felt relaxing. Too relaxing for someone who wanted to save Zoe.

"What's your name?" Iris thought she'd ask the girl.

"Call me 'servant,'" the girl said. "You're not supposed to know my name until..."

"Until?" Iris tilted her head.

"Again, I can't say."

"Well, that wasn't helpful," Iris rolled her eyes. "Can you tell me how the Beasts look, then?"

"I haven't seen one," the girl said. "I am a servant. I am not supposed to see my Masters. It's the polite way."

Although the massage was good, Iris was about to pull her hair out and scream. She needed to find a source of information, or get out of this room somehow.

"I bet you have an amazing steam bath somewhere," Iris said.

"The pool in your chamber does that."

"I meant a big pool, somewhere I can swim a long distance." Iris didn't give up.

"We do, but your Master hasn't allowed it yet."

It was obvious that the nameless girl was of no help. Iris had to take things in her own hands. She enjoyed her massage, and let the girl dress her and comb her hair in the mirror. Her hair seemed different. It seemed stiff again, like when she was a kid.

"That's strange," she told her servant. "Has my hair been that stiff since I came?"

"It's been horrible," the girl said, then looked like she regretted it. "I mean, no. I can fix it."

"You can be honest with me," Iris said. "I'm not going to bite you."

"Frankly, it's been like that."

"But I didn't have such bad hair in The Second." Iris said.

"Never?" the girl's voice peaked from under her veil.

"To tell the truth, I did when I was a kid. At least, I remember it was horrible. Although my mother always told me otherwise. She and my dad liked it a lot. Then somehow later, when I grew older, it seemed better."

"Maybe it's always been good," the girl said. "Maybe it was just your imagination."

"Could be," Iris sighed. Her hair was the last thing she cared about now. She had to get out of this chamber. She bowed forward suddenly and held her stomach, pretending it hurt badly. It was the oldest and cheesiest trick in the book, but she was out of options.

"Are you alright, My Beauty?" the girl looked worried.

"I think it's the food I ate," Iris growled.

"That's impossible," the girl said. "The food is the healthiest in the world."

"Could you at least get me a doctor?" Iris was losing it, frustrated she couldn't fool her servant. "You must have a doctor somewhere."

"We don't, My Beauty," the girl said. "No Bride ever gets ill here."

"How about the Masters?"

"I don't think they ever get sick," the girl snickered.

"What's so funny? I'm hurting here."

"You must just be imagining it," the girl said.

"Okay. That's it," Iris snapped. "I don't want you as a servant. Get out!" Iris couldn't control her anger. Repeatedly telling her how she really felt was getting on her nerves.

"As you wish, My Beauty," the girl showed no sign of anger. She obeyed her and walked to the wall, whispered to it as it turned into a door.

Iris had a fraction of a second to seize the opportunity. Fueled by her frustration, she dashed toward the door and knocked the girl to the floor. It was an unexpectedly hard hit. The girl fell, holding her head.

For a tiny second, Iris thought she'd pull her veil and see her face. It didn't sound like a good idea. Someone was going to come after Iris soon and she had to run.

48

Iris ran in the hallway with the stars beneath her feet. She ran faster than she thought she could. No one had come after her yet, but she knew it was inevitable. She didn't even know where to go, and what to do. The one thing that dawned on her was yelling Zoe's name.

"Zoe! Where are you? It's Iris. Please tell me you're alive!"

The white walls were misleading and suffocating. Iris realized her only guide were the stars. Men had been guided by stars all their lives, staring up at them and learning from them. Iris had them right beneath her feet. This must have been how Gods felt.

Finally, Iris came around to a huge opening to a newer place. There were no doors and no guards. Only a breathtaking scene like she had never imagined. She saw a vast green area with bending palm trees, swinging to the golden rays of a not-so-distant sun. She wasn't sure it was the same sun she saw on Earth. This one splayed the right amount of light and heat in a constant beam, never too warm or weak. The sky was pinkish, and void of stars. Rainbows were a dime a dozen. Birds on the tree sang actual songs, like humans did. Everything seemed to revolve around a certain spot: a waterfall.

What kind of ship was this, with a whole world inside it?

Iris ran down the slope toward this magnificent scene. She felt like a child again, running into her papa's arms. The feeling was so euphoric, that something inside her told her this wasn't real. It just couldn't be.

On her way down the slope, she saw there were way too many girls gathered down by the waterfall. They were swimming, singing, and laughing. And they were definitely human.

"Hey!" Iris shouted, walking barefoot on the wet grass. "Someone help me!"

The girls didn't pay attention to Iris. Their own content seemed to blind them from seeing the Bride escaping her chamber. Their movements were minimal, and they seemed hypnotized.

It dawned on Iris that these girls must have also been Brides. She'd found them. Finally.

As she ran, she was eager to see their faces. She'd recognize one or two for sure. Would she see Eva? Zoe, maybe? But she could only see their backs, as they sang and played happily in the water.

"Hey! Can't you hear me?" It was if she were invisible. "Did anyone see a girl named Zoe?"

Iris was only strides away from them, when her legs brought her to a stop. She thought one of the girls glanced at her briefly, then turned around. But it wasn't possible because this girl looked...

Iris lowered her head and stared at the grass. She didn't know why she did that, but she knew she was in for something horrible. Did she really see that? Was the girl's face real?

"I'm here Iris," a voice told her. It was calm, sad; and torn into pieces. So much so, she didn't recognize it was Zoe's in the beginning.

"Zoe?" Iris wondered, her head still lowered. "Is that you?"

"It's me, Iris. You have no idea what it means to me, you coming here for me."

"But Zoe," Iris was trembling. The girl's face she'd just seen was appalling. "I can't lift my head up to see you. I think I saw a girl who looked..."

"I know," Zoe's sad voice said. "I know what you have seen."

"Tell me they haven't done the same to you, Zoe," Iris said. "Please tell me you don't look like the girl I just saw."

Zoe didn't answer her. It was the only way to get Iris's curiosity to raise her head and look at her.

Iris raised her head slowly, hoping and praying she was wrong about what she had seen. She found Zoe was wearing an even brighter dress than hers. But that wasn't what Iris was afraid to look at. It was Zoe's face that was horrible. She looked so ugly, deformed, like it wasn't her face anymore. Even her hands looked the same way. Zoe looked like a monster. It was so grotesque and obscene, Iris couldn't comprehend how the Beasts had turned her into this shape. It was as if they'd performed a surgery on her to make her look that way.

"Who did this to you?" a scream escaped Iris's chest. "Did the Beasts do this to you?" she stepped forward and shook Zoe. "Why? Tell me. Why do they do this to the girls they take?"

"Just calm down, Iris." Zoe pleaded.

"I won't calm down. Don't be afraid of them. I will get you out of here."

"Please, calm down." Zoe repeated.

"Remember when you told me to avenge you as you got on the ship?" Iris said, tears flooding from her eyes. "I swear, I'll make them pay. Just answer me. Did the Beasts do this to you?" Iris's face reddened, pondering the unimaginable possibilities. Did the Beasts envy human beauty, so they destroyed it? Were they experimenting on humans like lab rats? "Did Andre do that to you? Is that what he is going to do to me when my time comes?" Iris followed.

"There has been a horrible war, Iris," Zoe said, tears trickling down her face. She sounded like Andre, answering a question with irrelevant thoughts.

"What?" Iris's puzzled pupils grew bigger.

"A horrible war in The First," Zoe said. "It destroyed everything on Earth. Everything," she stressed. "Our ancestors, the few of them who survived, were left with deficiencies, diseases, and illnesses."

"Why are you telling me that, Zoe?" Iris wondered.

"It was nuclear war. The skies turned gray. The plants died. And the animals turned into sick monsters," Zoe recited a story that seemed so important to her. "Just like the Ruins where you practiced your Pentimento."

"Listen to me, Zoe," Iris shook her harder. "You're hallucinating. They drugged you. It's the red rose. I can help you."

"I'm not hallucinating," Zoe pushed her arms away, crying even harder. "Our ancestors didn't look pretty. It was the aftermath of the radiation. They weren't capable of bringing normal offspring to the world."

"Offspring?" Iris couldn't help but finally listen to Zoe. She'd never seen Zoe so insistent on speaking her own mind. What did she mean by offspring?

"Yes. Offspring. Us," Zoe said. "We've never been cured. We've never been the humans we think we are. We've never been beautiful. We've always been the Beasts."

49

Before Zoe could explain further, the girls in white forcefully dragged Iris back to her room. She tried her best to free herself, but they buzzed her with their weapons.

"Ouch!" Iris cried out. The pain of their instruments were suddenly intolerable, or was it the shock of what Zoe had just told her?

Iris couldn't help but think that the Beasts tampered with Zoe's brain. Zoe had been susceptible to hallucinations since her accident, when she thought that Colton was one of the Beasts. But why did the Beasts hurt her so much? Why deform her this way?

Master Andre was waiting for Iris in her chamber. The white girls bowed their heads and stood behind her as he sat on a chair, covered in a white veil.

"Leave us alone," Andre waved his gloved hands. The girls complied immediately and left.

"What have you done to Zoe?" Iris gritted her teeth and ran into him, hitting and kicking his tall and strong frame. Andre stood up, held her by the arms, and pushed her with her back against the wall. The green scary eyes watched her from behind the veil. Iris hated herself for continuously feeling this attraction toward him. He'd hurt all those girls and did these horrible things to their faces. He'd hurt Zoe. And Iris still felt like she wanted to crash into his arms. What kind of person was she?

How. Could. She?

Andre said nothing. He had his grip firm on her, and waited calmly, until every pore in her skin eventually gave in to his masculine dominance. She thought he was enjoying his power over her. The silent, almost godly, power of the Beast. It occurred to her that the Beasts must be an only-male species. That explained it all. The girls were only slaves, and the Beasts needed to produce children and save their species. Maybe they needed love. The kind of love only a woman could provide. That must have been it. Of all conclusions, this was most sound to her. But why hurt the girl who could grant you the love you needed? And why mess with her mind?

Why did Zoe say we're the Beasts? Why?

Iris tried one last kick at Andre, throbbing like a dying fish. Then, when she finally realized he was much stronger than her, she did what she had no memory of doing ever before. She cried for the first time since her mother's death.

"Surrendering isn't a bad thing." Andre said. It puzzled her how soothing his voice was, comforting in the strangest ways.

"I don't want to surrender," she sobbed.

"Sometimes we have to in order to see."

"See and clear my head," she said. "All this crap you try to feed me. All this crap you fed Zoe's head." Andre softened his grip on her, and she let her hands slide as she knelt down on the floor. "What did you do to her? Why do you take girls from The Second? Why girls? What kind of animals are you?"

"Girls are the flower of life," Andre knelt next to her. So close, she wished she could see his face now. "Men can conquer, build, and perform. But they can't give birth. They can't nurture. They can't seed love. Love might be something they can give, but can't incept."

"Is that what it's all about?" she stared at him behind the veil. "You need babies... and... love?"

Andre's silence should have driven her crazy. Instead, she cried some more. Was it possible that whatever Zoe said was true? That they were the real Beasts? In what sense? This couldn't be. "Show me your face," she demanded, drying her tears. "Show me your face, now!"

"Do you think you are ready to see it?" Andre said. Iris discarded his words and nodded. She had to see it at all costs now. She had to prove to herself that he was a Beast, she had to make sure Zoe's words were just hallucinations. This was what all of this was about. This was the big Pentimento moment, when she was about to see how the Beasts who ruled them truly looked.

"As you wish, Iris." Andre stood up and took a few steps back. Iris stood up with her back against the window with the stars. She could hear him breathing heavily underneath the veil. She saw him lift his hands to his veil, but then stopped hesitantly. "Would you like to pull the veil down yourself?" he said.

Iris didn't say yes. She just walked toward him, tilted her head up to meet his chin and tiptoed to pull it down.

50

Andre looked like Zoe, horrendous in every which way. At least Zoe looked like a damaged human being. Andre was far from it. He was a freak of nature.

The most tolerable feature in his face were his green eyes, which looked a bit yellowish, like a demon's. It was hard to tell cheek from ears and mouth from chin in his face. The Beasts looked pathetic.

"No wonder you hide your ugliness from us," Iris said. "None of us would've followed a Beast's order if we had seen what you look like."

"So you think I am ugly?" Andre said.

"Ugly? Are you kidding me?" she shook her shoulders. "Grotesque is a compliment to your kind."

"I've been called worse. In the beginning."

"What is that supposed to mean? You think I could love you if I spent more time with you? If I got used to what you look like?" Iris said.

Andre, like usual, spared his words. This time, Iris wasn't frustrated with him. His ugliness was a relief in many ways—although her heart had really wished he wasn't. It lessened her attraction toward him--or what she'd had felt initially--and it proved to her Zoe's talk was just hallucination.

Iris turned around and looked at the beautiful stars, wondering why such a beautiful world would be owned by such ugly Beasts. At the end of her stare she saw a memory. It was of her learning about Pentimento in her father's basement as a kid. A wonderful memory, one that had only shaped her mind. Only this time, she remembered one day when she had woken up late at night and decided to sneak one last peak at the Beast in

Fragonard's painting. That night something strange happened. When she inspected the painting underneath, the boy wasn't a Beast. He was unearthly beautiful. Iris rubbed her eyes, and then the image was gone. The boy was a Beast again. Her eyes must have been playing games on her. She must have wished the boy to be beautiful so bad, her mind had granted her that illusion for a fraction of a second.

Yes. It was an illusion, she told herself now, because the ugly Beast in Fragonard's painting was Andre.

51

Zoe had been pleading to meet Prince Andre in private for some time. Since Iris had arrived, he'd been busy with her. It was no secret that he'd been deeply in love with Iris since the first time he'd laid eyes on her. It was a critical situation for the prince, since the king and queen of their world would have never allowed a beautiful man like him to couple with an "ugly" from The Second.

Andre had promised Zoe answers when she first came, but he'd said he'd do that after Iris knew who, and what, she was. Now that Iris wasn't capable of seeing what the stars really were, Zoe thought the Prince owed her explanations. Finally, she was led to the prince's chamber, where he awaited her with hands laced behind his back.

"Zoe." He bowed his head with respect. "What can I do for you?"

"You promised me answers, My Prince," she said, secretly envying his unearthly beauty. She'd learned it was better for him never to descend to The Second, or the girls would go crazy.

"I did, indeed," he said. "Please, sit down. I'll have to make it brief, though. You know I need to watch Iris most of the day."

"How is she now?" Zoe sat opposite to him.

"Still not seeing the stars," Andre sighed, and sat down. "She's a stubborn girl."

"But you like her stubbornness," Zoe nodded her head slightly.

"You're right. One should accept the person they love for who they are," he tapped his hands on his lap. "It's just that the king and queen are on the verge of wanting to get rid of her."

"But you will not let that happen, right?" Zoe was worried. She loved Iris more than anything, and although she knew the truth would be shocking to her, she hoped she'd find it out sooner, rather than later.

"I'm not going to let anyone hurt her, Zoe. You know that. I'll fight the world for her," Andre's seriousness almost intimidated Zoe, but it was one of his best traits. He was such a strong young man. "Now, ask me and I shall answer you," he said.

"First of all, is The Second totally destroyed in reality?" she asked.

"The Second is just what's left from the horrible war from the days of The First United States of America," Andre said. "It's no different from the Ruins. All people inhabiting it are suffering from deformations from that war."

"Then how is it we don't see it, or the world around us, for what it really is?" Zoe wondered. "I know you have explained this before, but I need to know more. I can't register it in my mind."

"It's not easy for you to imagine it. I mean humans have been living a lie for so long. It will take some time to sink in, just like the idea of the red Indians not seeing Columbus's ships at first," Andre said. "When the war in The First destroyed everything, humans had to live with their deformed looks for ages. It was devastating. There was no hope in the world, and no reasons motivated them to build The Second. A number of humans, who were scientists and politicians before, needed to solve the problem with human looks after the radiation. They realized that the people needed to believe they were beautiful, even if it was a lie."

"So they invented the…"

"The Pentimento, yes," Andre said. "Not the Pentimento as an artistic term, but the Pentimento as in an illusion of technology that changed harsh realities into sweeter ones in the eyes of humans. The Pentimento is a small wiring installed in the human brain, right behind the eyes. It makes a human see everything the way they'd want to see it. The technology had been invented in the last days of the First, before the world was destroyed."

"But the technology survived?"

"The transcripts and how to use it did," Andre nodded. "Only no one had ever used it, until the Council showed up. They were Americans, wanting to rebuild the world their ancestors destroyed. They designed the Pentimento so no one would see how deformed they looked. Or how the world looked. Thus, giving them motivation to live. In the end, they discovered that *'humans only see what they want to see, where they are in their minds, who they want to be.'*"

"So we live in some sort of a virtual reality in The Second," Zoe said absently. "Only we're not sleeping in cells, or imagining it. We're actually seeing it through our fake eyes."

"It's an unimaginable technology to you, I know," Andre said. "But we've seen it for a long time. When you walk into a building, it's damaged, but you don't see it. You look at someone, they are ugly, but you also don't see it. At some point the program took on a life of its own, and realities became consistent in every human brain in The Second. The way you saw Iris's looks was the same way Cody saw her. And the world moved on. Call it evolution of the imagination, if you like."

"So, we're all brainwashed to believe the same lie?" Zoe said absently.

"However," Andre leaned forward in his chair. "Sometimes glitches occur, like when you thought Colton was the Beast."

"I don't actually remember it, but everyone says I did." Zoe said. "Are you saying my eyes suddenly saw him for who he really was, an ugly human like all of us?" Zoe wasn't comfortable with calling humans ugly. She just didn't know any other way to describe it.

"Exactly. You had a terrible accident and trauma at Vera's birthday party. Sometimes, accidents mess with the system, and you were able to see how the world around you really looks for a brief moment. In your case, everyone thought you were hallucinating because of the medicine, and you ended up not remembering it."

"That's why you have Fragonard's painting here in your chamber--and Picasso's? It's never been actually in Iris's father's possession, was it?" Zoe said, connecting the dots.

"True." Andre nodded. "It's hard to explain, but the Pentimento technology stems its memories from your ancestors, then evolves when you grow up. Iris's father comes from a family that was obsessed with the idea of Pentimentos in paintings. He inherited the idea in his mind about a painting with an earlier version buried underneath. His mind cherished the idea, and his eyes, through the crazy technology of illusion, granted him things that weren't there. Of course, Iris was capable of seeing the Fragonard painting too, because of the collective conscience the technology created. If you're a child and your parents tell you a lion doesn't bite, you're likely to believe them at first. Like I said, the program took a life of its own, and everyone was living the same unreal life in The Second."

"And the Ruins?"

"The Ruins act as our qualifier, of sorts." Andre said. "My race is as old as the sun. We travel the galaxy in our ships, and don't have a home. We look like humans, but we aren't. As you see, we're actually much better looking."

"Then why did the Earth interest you?"

"Frankly, it doesn't interest everyone. The king and queen think the human race is horrible. Unredeemable in every way." Andre sighed. "Some of us thought otherwise. Next to the stupidity that drove a man to destroy his own world, small traits like passion and love seemed to be interesting, and different from other species. But what really caught our eyes was the denial humans live in. Denial seems like a favorite trait. The way you invented the Pentimento technology so you could not look at your own ugliness, that's something I have never seen in any other race."

"What do other races do?"
"They face the reality of who they are, and work on it from there," Andre said. "But like I said, humans…"

"…only see what they want to see." Zoe nodded. She wasn't proud of it in any way. The deformed face she had to live with was nothing compared to the shame she felt as a human now. "I still don't get why you designed the Ruins," she wondered.

"The Ruins are how the world outside of the program really was. We arrested your Council and created the Ruins in the virtual reality, so we could spot people who'd be curious about it."

"Like Iris?"

"And like almost every Bride we took," Andre said. "We created loopholes in The Second so the few humans who were ready to face their reality, those who liked to question, those who were willing to change, would surface, and then we could spot them."

"And pretend to be taking them as Brides," Zoe finished his thought.

"Exactly," Andre said. "The Bride system was in itself a loophole. It was utterly unbelievable humans gave in to such a horrid system. They didn't question it, didn't fight it, and only wished they weren't next. Those who questioned it finally, like you and Iris, actually become our Brides."

"So the Brides were just you choosing the girls who rebelled against the system," Zoe said. "I understand that, but why not boys?"

"We are going to take boys soon. We have a list." Andre said. "Women were just our priority."

"Why?"

"Believe or not, the world needs women more than men. Think of a train that's about to explode. Who would you save first?"

"Women and children first," Zoe mumbled.

"You get the point," Andre bowed his head. "Is there anything else you need to ask me?"

"In fact, yes," she said. "Why are you collecting women and men into your ship? Why, when they are still ugly and deformed from the radiation's aftermaths?"

"To build what you might want to call The Third," Andre said. "With real people, without denial, and without lies. Collect the greatest minds, the most passionate and good-hearted people, and start a new world, on an island maybe. Let them start like the Stone Age man. Let them hunt, fish, and seed the earth all over again. Let them forget about their looks, and expose themselves to their Pentimento, to become the best they can. Let them cherish how humanity started, and love how evolutionary things became."

"I would have never thought I'd say this, but I'm actually honored you have chosen me to be part of The Third." Zoe said. "It means I am a good human. I like that."

"Humans aren't bad, Zoe," Andre said. "They are just stupid."

"But Eva and Elia weren't rebellious girls. Why them?" Zoe said.

Andre laughed. "You're right about that." He said. "Well, that would be the king and queen's suggestion."

"Why would they suggest that?"

"The queen believes that good in people isn't absolute, that good is only *good* when challenged. Eva and Elia, and the like, will be part of The Third to create the balance the world needs. A little bit of human stupidity and annoyance, to balance the whole."

"So basically, your race is looking to help us and give us a second chance," Zoe said.

"A third." Andre joked. "And frankly, even if we have to go as far as the tenth chance, we'll wait. I believe in humans." Andre pulled out a silver device, and pressed a button on it. A screen showed Iris in her room, standing on the glass floor with what she thought were the stars underneath. "I believe in humans," he repeated. "Or how did I end up falling in love with one?" Andre's eyes twinkled seeing Iris.

Zoe shared his gaze at Iris in her chamber, kneeling down and looking at the stars.

They weren't stars at all.

They were chunks of burned ball-like clouds hanging in the sky, an aftermath of the war in The First. They looked gray and crusted, like a burnt cookie. It was an unpleasant sight. The whole Earth beyond the stars was a foam of gray, too, blocking the sun from reaching through. This was nothing like the Earth's photographs taken from space; those pictures they saw in The Second of how beautiful the Earth was.

"I think it will take Iris a long time to realize what she is looking at," Andre said.

"Why do you think that, Prince Andre?" Zoe felt saddened for her friend.

"Unexpectedly, Iris's denial is supreme. The wiring behind her eyes prevents her from seeing the real world around her. She even thought I was ugly when I showed her my face."

"Can't you just pull the wiring and show her the real world?"

"I could," Andre considered. "But then she has to be sent back to The Second. We only believe in those who *see* the truth on their own. I provided her with the towel which loosens the Pentimento's effect. I talked to her and massaged her brain. I showed her I own Fragonard's real painting. And I told stories about perception, like when the Red Indians first saw Christopher Columbus. Unlike other Brides, these techniques never worked with her. She has to see what the stars really are eventually. I can't lose her," Andre's voice weakened, and Zoe wondered if Iris ever knew how blessed she was, with Andre loving her unconditionally like that.

"But don't you think it's strange? I mean, she saw me as deformed as I am," Zoe said, watching Iris tap her foot against the glass, wondering what she was supposed to see. It was clear she still thought of them as stars.

"That's probably because she cares a lot about you, and you're her best friend. I can't deny that it's partial progress, but why didn't she see me, or the stars?" Andre said. "I mean, Iris is one of the most intelligent girls. One of the most passionate. She is a fighter. A lover. She defied us, sent the red roses to the parents of the Brides. Hell, she stood on the top of the world, challenging our invincible and powerful race. She has an unstoppable faith in the Pentimento. It's in her nature to question things, to see what lies beneath the *lies*. Why can't she see the stars for what they are?" Andre lost his temper and slammed his hand on his chair.

Zoe sympathized with him, the same way she sympathized with Iris. Of all people, it didn't make sense that Iris didn't see the truth about the stars. It didn't make sense her eyes hadn't been entranced by Prince Andre's beauty. She wondered how that was possible.

"Wait!" Andre said, pointing at Iris kneeling down to the glass, and wiping it with a towel.

"You think she finally saw it?" Zoe chirped.

"Let's see."

Iris wiped the glass a couple of times, as if trying to see clearly behind it. When it cleared, she locked her gaze downward for a long time. Andre and Zoe's breathing tightened, longing for the moment she saw the truth. Iris was still looking and looking. Her gaze was expressionless. Did she see the world for what it really was?

Finally, Iris stood up and waved her hands in the air. "They're just stars beneath my feet."

52

Colton was losing it. He could not believe Iris challenged the Beast, and was taken so easily. How could she not consult him? He knew she was stubborn and impulsive, and he actually liked these traits in her. But how could she? He thought he'd found the love of his life here in The Second.

He was digging like crazy into the soil of the Ruins. Hours and hours of being alone in this world wasn't helping him. He needed to do this. No family, friends, cars, or looks filled the void Iris left behind.

"Stupid, Iris. Why did you do this? I can't live here on my own. This world seems so fake, and you were the only thing that made it right. You were that rock that stabilized my life, and gave meaning to it." Colton dug the shovel elsewhere.

The Ruins were gloomy, like always. He was searching for something only Iris was capable of finding. But he was determined to get it tonight.

Dig here. Dig there. Look for it everywhere.

Finally, he found what he was looking for. He tucked it in his pocket, and ran away to leave the Ruins.

Half an hour later, he was in his car, speeding up through the city, running traffic lights, and not caring in the least. He pushed the gas pedal and saw only Iris's face in the horizon. She was so far away. So far away.

Colton stopped in front of the Sinai Tower and got out of his car. He convinced the guards he was here on behalf of his father, got through, and took the elevator up to the roof.

The police had set a number of guards on the rooftop. Androids like those who guard the schools. But nothing was going to stop Colton. Nothing.

"I am walking toward the guards," he called Cody on the phone.

"Roger that, bro," Cody replied. Colton heard him click some buttons on his keyboard. A moment later, the guards froze like machines. "It's clear now," Cody said. "But hurry. You only got two minutes before they wake up."

"Thanks bro," Colton said, and walked toward the center.

Suddenly, a guard showed up in front of him. The police had left a human behind.

Colton didn't hesitate. He punched him in the face instantly. The man was strong though, and punched back. "You should really leave," Colton told him. "The energy I got in my heart is much stronger than anything you have seen."

The policeman grinned at the young boy's foolishness. Sadly, it was his last grin in a long time. Colton punched him again, drawing out a tooth. Then he followed with another punch that knocked the man down.

"That's my bro!" Cody clapped on the phone.

Colton walked to the middle of the rooftop and took a deep breath.

"Ready, Colton?" Cody said.

"I am." He pulled out the red rose he'd finally picked up from the Ruins, and watched it with eager eyes. He smelled it for a moment with closed eyes.

"It's time." Cody said.

"You need anything from up there, bro?" Colton joked, disguising his fears.

"How about you bring Zoe back with Iris," Cody said. "You know I'd have joined you, if I hadn't had that awful cold all week."

Colton laughed. "Anything else?" he said, staring at the stars in the sky, those glittering stars separating him from Iris.

"Don't forget to write," Cody said.

"I won't need to," Colton said. "I'll be back soon. It's only stars separating me from Zoe and Iris. How bad could it be?" Colton gazed at the stars again. "Damn, Iris. Now I literally have to go to the moon and back to be with you." He raised the red rose, defying the Beasts' sovereign, in the air. If they took the challenge, he'd be the first boy to ever be taken by the Beasts, willingly or not.

53

Miles and miles away from Colton, up in space, Iris sat cross-legged on the glass floor above the stars. She had requested an old painting to practice her Pentimento hobby. Prince Andre was kind enough to grant her this wish. She'd been here for seven days, doing nothing but sitting here and working with the paintings.

Iris knew the Beasts were watching her; those ugly Beasts trying to persuade her that her whole world was a lie, and asking her to look at the stars.

Even Zoe visited her a couple of times, talking in codes and riddles, hinting at things. Zoe said she loved Iris so much, she'd die for her. It was true. And Iris would have done the same. Hell, she'd already done it by defying the Beasts for her.

Still, Iris told Zoe that all she could see were the beautiful stars.

Iris, now alone in her chamber, pushed the painting aside and stood up. She lowered her head and gazed down at the glass floor, pulling the hem of her wedding dress slightly up. She did it as if she were about to dance. Somewhere far below was the place she came from; where she met Colton Ray.

She had no idea that at this very moment, Colton was holding a red rose up and defying the Beasts, only to be with her. But somehow, in a rare and exclusively human emotion, she could feel Colton's presence, as if he were near without even *seeing* him.

She didn't need much explanation or knowledge to analyze her feelings. They were just there, and looking down at the galaxy made her feel a star or two closer to him. *How many light years were those?*

Even if her attraction to Andre was unearthly, her heart belonged to Colton. He was the one she had always wanted. Her first kiss. The only one she'd dreamed of growing old with. And maybe have kids. And ironically die with, and be buried next to.

True, they might give birth to deformed kids, as ugly looking as she and Colton really were. But it didn't matter. She didn't need an alien race to tell her how to deal with her human problems. As ugly as they were, she and Colton could work it out. They had to work it out. It's what their humanity was all about.

The first time she'd realized what she really was while on the ship was shocking. But then she comprehended it had never been about the looks. The strength humans can show and the stars humans can cross were in themselves unearthly traits. If the beautiful aliens wanted to judge them, they should try living on Earth first, get on their knees and see a plant, feed a dog, or raise kids. Then we'd see how long they'd survive.

Iris knelt to the floor again with her bare feet. She stretched an arm out to touch the glass, looking at the gray skies and the burned stars with a broad smile on her face. It wasn't a beautiful sight at first, but it did hold a beautiful dream at the end of her gaze: Colton. She could feel him down there somewhere, waiting for her.

And in this precise moment, Iris had an epiphany, that Colton at the end of her gaze, beyond the burned stratosphere, was her Pentimento.

Hold on, Colton. She thought. *I'm coming for you. If I keep insisting that I still see the stars, they'll want to get rid of me and send me back to The Second. Stay strong.*

The END...

Want Iris's, Colton's, and Andre's story to continue?

Just visit: www.Cameronjace.com *and enter your email. You'll get personal updates from me. I promise you'll be the first* to know when Book Two is released! But here is the thing; my lovely beta readers had different opinions on this ending. Some thought, like me, that the story ends here with an open ended scene. And some encouraged me to continue it and write book 2, which should be called *Stars Beneath Her Feet.* I will leave that up to you to decide. So if you think there should be a second book, don't miss out: www.cameronjace.com

Entering your email will also notify you of any other books I write when they come out. Plus you can check facts like the Fragonard paiting and real life Pentimentos in my emails.

Thank you so much for reading.

Merry Christmas and happy holidays,

Cameron Jace

Made in the USA
Lexington, KY
03 July 2016